Wicked Spirits Dethroned
By Joseph Daeges

Wicked Spirits Dethroned by Joseph Daeges
Copyright © 2020. All rights reserved.

ALL RIGHTS RESERVED: No part of this book may be reproduced, stored, or transmitted, in any form, without the express and prior permission in writing of Pen It! Publications. This book may not be circulated in any form of binding or cover other than that in which it is currently published.

This book is licensed for your personal enjoyment only. All rights are reserved. Pen It! Publications does not grant you rights to resell or distribute this book without prior written consent of both Pen It! Publications and the copyright owner of this book. This book must not be copied, transferred, sold or distributed in any way.

Disclaimer: Neither Pen It! Publications, or our authors will be responsible for repercussions to anyone who utilizes the subject of this book for illegal, immoral or unethical use.

This is a work of fiction. The views expressed herein do not necessarily reflect that of the publisher.

This book or part thereof may not be reproduced in any form, stored in a retrieval system, or transmitted in any form by any means-electronic, mechanical, photocopy, recording or otherwise-without prior written consent of the publisher, except as provided by United States of America copyright law.

Published by Pen It! Publications, LLC
812-371-4128   www.penitpublications.com

ISBN: 978-1-952011-25-2
Cover by Pen It! Publications, LLC
Edited by Peggy Holt and Jen Selinsky

Contents

Chapter 1: A Cottage for Sale 1
Chapter 2: A Happy Family 15
Chapter 3: A Mysterious Lantern 27
Chapter 4: Taking the First Step 33
Chapter 5: PETRONAS 45
Chapter 6: Crime 57
Chapter 7: Appearance of the Doll 83
Chapter 8: Claude's Family Victimized 101
Chapter 9: Trailing the Doll 115
Chapter 10: PETRONAS at War 131
Chapter 11: The Curse Is Broken 163
Chapter 12: The Reward 179

Chapter 1
A Cottage for Sale

After their working day was complete, residents of a small farmer's town in Spain reunited with their families at home and enjoyed a beautiful ending to the evening. A deep sense of peace, and unison, was always felt by all its inhabitants. Foremost, it was a quiet town in Ronda, where there was only traffic light, and the overall mood was peaceful.

All that was just about to change because of some speculation that one of the houses in the neighborhood was haunted. The cause had yet to be determined. Visitors to town could not tell the difference between one house and another. But those who lived there knew perfectly well. No resident of the town was willing to step into the cottage.

Paranormal experts were called on occasion, privately, of course, to try to unveil the source of the problematic situation. So far, no one was capable of determining the real cause of the paranormal curse.

The property included a mansion, and the splendid, lovable cottage, which one had the heart to destroy. Some villagers were suspicious that, if the cottage was to be demolished, then it would create other problems.

At town meetings, questions concerning what to do with the cottage was a constant subject. There were no officials who were willing to step up to render the final decision whether to demolish it, or wait and see if anything else happened.

Some of the town officials had tried to buy the cottage, but were forced out not long after they purchased it. There were hundreds of rituals performed in the hope of curbing the disturbance that the cottage was causing to the town.

Nothing was effective, until one day; someone discovered a manuscript left in the library. The document was kept confidential because of the personal information that it contained. Many town officials were aware of the manuscript, but no one was willing to touch it.

It was as if the document, itself, was possessed by a spirit; just one look at the cover was enough to provoke anxiety, and wonder.

For a long period of time, the town officials decided just to leave the cottage abandoned, condemned to grow wild. That avenue was not the perfect one but, every time someone was tasked with cleaning it, or caring for it, they came home with some strange, short-term illnesses.

The cottage stood, like a ghost, reminding every inhabitant of the town about the strange, and unpredictable, events it was responsible for.

One day, the town hall officials received a call from a foreigner who was interested in buying the cottage. The man was surprised that no one in the town was willing to occupy it.

It was a dilemma for the city officials about how to handle the request because of all the prior incidents. The few times the cottage was sold, the city was cited in court for not having disclosed potential issues that the cottage was plagued with.

The city lost the cases and had to pay the owner damages, plus court costs. The question was how to present a disclosure concerning the problem coming from the cottage without divulging *all* the personal information.

That morning, the atmosphere in the town hall was heavy among the city officials. No one was willing to set up contact with the potential new owner to inform him about the problematic situation. The idea of taking the cottage off the market had been considered, and it was a possibility.

For now, it was still for sale, and they had a potential buyer; that would make easier for the city because they would not need to send someone to clean the exterior of the cottage.

On that morning, the decision was made to let the potential new owner possess the cottage.

Just before the meeting, the foreigner had called to see if he could at least set up an appointment to take a look at the cottage.

That delicate mission was given to the best realtor in town, in the hope that the potential owner would back down and choose another avenue. He was told to make the place as miserable-looking as possible, citing the list of bad experiences, and the cost of maintaining the property, as well as the property taxes.

A time was set for the foreigner, who was named Claude, to come look at the cursed cottage which he wanted to purchase. He was greeted by the realtor at the gate of the cottage.

After a brief handshake, the conversation fell to the cottage. The foreigner wanted to know how many acres it had because, when he read the realtor's ad, it was not disclosed. It had the potential buyer left at odds, and he was curious as to why it was not stated in the listing. The realtor was a little amused with the last inquiry of the potential buyer and told him that it was a mistake.

He was happy to tell Claude that the cottage came with one hundred and twenty acres. As for the price, the realtor told the potential buyer that, since it was such a small community, it affected the price. The realtor tried to sell it as a beautiful, charming cottage with lots of potential, the opposite of what he was told to do.

Claude stepped into the cottage. It was time to see what else the property had to offer. They were two barns and a garage, also a wooden shed. The outsides of the buildings were kept in good shape by the city workers.

Claude was keen to see the interior of the barn. The realtor did not want to sound the alarm, so he mustered his courage and entered the barn with the potential buyer. Everything inside was in good shape, ready for use.

They took a little walk around the property to see what else there was. The natural ambience, and serenity, made the foreigner fall for it.

"Just give me the price tag of this lovable cottage," Claude said.

To his request, the specialist gave the actual price tag; it was listed for one hundred fifty thousand dollars. He countered with one hundred twenty-five thousand dollars.

He sensed the realtor's hesitation and said, "I will pay cash."

The realtor nodded. "Well, I think we could make a deal."

They walked back into the mansion, where they sat at the kitchen table.

Some brief conversation took place, and the foreigner asked why no one else was interested in occupying the cottage. It was surprising to see the place so well taken care of, and he suspected that there was some sort of escrow attached to the property.

The realtor assured him that there were no attachments. If he was to buy the mansion, the cottage, and everything else on the grounds, would be his.

He added that he had all the documentation at city hall and that, if Claude wanted, he could produce it to him at a specific time.

That answer had given some reassurance to the foreigner about the sale of the cottage.

"What about tomorrow morning at nine o'clock? Would this work for you?"

"Yes, it will definitely work for me. In the meantime, I will put money down to ensure that no one else gets the cottage."

To this, the realtor asked Claude if he had some children, which concerned Claude greatly. "Why do you need to know this?"

The realtor replied that the cottage was under an inexplicable curse; that was the reason for the great bargain. "I am telling you, this beautiful place had many new owners, and everyone had left the place with some dissatisfaction. Most of them even sued the city."

Upon hearing this information, Claude replied, "You do not have to worry about that. I am an expert in paranormal matters. I have to admit that I already sensed a weird presence while walking to the barn." Claude added that he had felt a stronger presence upon first entering the first barn and that, maybe, it was the source of the dilemma.

The realtor became more at ease with the proposition, and the sale, as the conversation took a different avenue.

"Are you telling me that you have the knowledge, and the capacity, to deal with this haunted cottage?"

"I sure do. I have already dealt with situations where no one had been able to succeed."

Again, the realtor insisted to know if the future owner of the cottage had any children. He explained that the situation was always worse when there were children involved.

Claude replied, "Sure, I do have children, but they grew up with paranormal activity."

"And nothing bad happened to them?"

"Not anything bad happened to them. I prepared them way before the event and, in many circumstances, they came out victorious, even faster than I did."

"Let me tell you, this cottage is nothing close to what you have already seen, especially if you have children involved. The whole story, by itself, is scary, and disgusting, because of the nature of the aftermath of the attack by the will of this evil spirit."

"My children are the best of the best when it comes time to confronting such spooky encounters."

The realtor was in disbelief upon hearing the proud father's tone of voice.

The conversation then turned to if the children were doing this by free will, or if they were forced to adapt to situations imposed on them.

Claude replied, "Really, ghost stories did not influence the life they've had. As a matter of fact, ghost stories are only as believable as you put your faith into them. Most likely, all the evidence I've accumulated over the years came from active imaginations rather than actual ghosts."

The realtor jumped in. "I assure you, the whole town is not making up these stories. I, myself, tried to buy this lovely cottage."

"I know I touched a nerve. Let me make myself clear. I am not putting down anyone in this town. I am just saying, having seen and experienced other presumed haunted houses, that I became skeptical of those claims of hauntings."

"Well, that is your opinion," replied the realtor.

After that conversation, a tense moment was felt, and ideas ran across the minds of both men.

The realtor knew that the cottage very well because he loved the place but, after many attempts to overcome the ghost residing there, he was forced to pack up and leave it behind.

The realtor took Claude to a lovely little island which was part of the cottage. There, he pointed out that he had started to build a little cabin for summertime.

"Something bad happened there?" Claude asked. "I sense some horrible activities took place in this isolated island."

The proud realtor replied, "Well, perhaps, you say that because you, too, have an active imagination."

Claude replied, "Oh, you took my observation too much to heart. Many of these places have come to be pure illusion, mixed with the need for attention."

After that exchange, the realtor and the expert were on their way exploring what else the property had to offer. They arrived at the water well.

The expert could sense that some powerful waves were coming out onto the surface. He looked at the realtor and said, "This is definitely a point of interest into the discovery of the horrible activity that took place in this cottage."

The realtor nervously said, "I just now remember, while I was the owner of this cottage, I reported this area to the police."

"I wonder, if by doing so, you would have jeopardized the whole investigation. I also notice that, in many cases, law enforcement is called too fast. This led to the destruction of some critical clues left behind by the wise perpetrator. I would suggest, for now, that you ignore my findings."

"Is there anything else you sense from this well?" asked the curious realtor.

"No," replied Claude.

"You are the first person who I showed this place to that really came up with good information, and was capable of pinpointing a least the potential problem," said the realtor.

"Yes, I suppose many buyers come and go but, now, this will be history because I sense that I am the one who will bring order, and control, over this grim situation."

The ecstatic realtor said, "Maybe, after you deal with the phenomenon haunting this cottage, you would be willing to sell it to me. I would ensure that the history, and the events that took place here, would never come to a forgotten past."

Claude had a good laugh and replied, "Sure, I would sell it to you. This would give me a couple more bucks for this beautiful place."

The realtor replied, "Maybe we could cut a deal we would agree both on. After all, I already owned this cottage, I had to give it up because of problematic supernatural forces."

"Okay, enough for now; let's continue our discovery. We have already been in this lovely place for four hours. We should talk about business, like setting up the contact of agreement to buy the cottage."

"Yes, I suppose you would be the right person to acquire this wonderful cottage," said the realtor.

After a brief moment of recollection, the two men were on their way to their cars.

Once he had taken one last look at the wonderful land, the expert was already was forming his plan of action. Once in his car, the realtor gave a signal to the expert to follow him to the town hall.

Slowly, they both were on their way to the town hall to complete the sale.

***

They arrived at the courthouse but, unfortunately, it was past business hours; living in a small town had his ups and downs.

Claude had to wait till the next day to purchase the cottage. A little deceived, he drove back to his house, where he let his loved ones know that he had bought a new home for the family.

Claude anticipated the early morning hours of the next day.

***

That next morning, Claude was on the road toward the promised land. At precisely 9:00, the transaction began at the courthouse; it took a couple of hours. Eventually, the deal was closed, and the key of the cottage was handed over to the new owner.

The realtor shook Claude's hand and welcomed him, and his family, to their new community.

Claude replied, "For now, I must get down to business. You are always welcome if you have time to come help me in my discoveries. I am sure that I can use some of your insight, and your help."

"Thank you for inviting me. I will see what I can do to help you. I will make every effort to be there when time permits."

"Not so fast. Remember, you are dealing with an adversary whom you could not defeat by yourself." After having said that, however, the realtor apologized, and the sale was complete.

The joyous expert in paranormal situations became the new legal owner of the haunted cottage. "Now, it is time for me to get down to business. I just can't wait to uncover what this cottage has to reveal," Claude said as

Chapter 2
A Happy Family

The first thing Claude did was to change all the locks of the mansion, and the adjunct buildings. He was proud of his accomplishment at having acquired such a wonderful cottage.

Claude was driving back to his family's prime residence; a joyful father was getting ready to announce the good news to the rest of the family.

He arrived with a smile so wide that his wife was taken by surprise. She knew that her husband was in the process of acquiring a new property, but she did not know all the details. He proudly announced the news at the dinner table once they were all united as a family.

Everyone seemed to be happy about the good news, and they were looking forward to the weekend when they would visit the newly acquired property.

That night, just before going to bed, Claude sat at the table kitchen with his wife, and they talked about the possibilities of the purchase. That was when Claude revealed to her that the cottage had a history of being haunted.

Sophia was not surprised. After all, this was Claude's livelihood. She was rather happy that her husband had found some work. She knew that he would soon take control of whatever situation was going on in the cottage. They would have a boost in their finances as a result. For now, it was time to make the necessary plans.

In the morning, Claude would drive to the library to see if there was any guidance left by any prior owners. After he hugged and kissed his wife, Claude started planning for tomorrow.

His four children slept soundly: Julian, the fourteen-year-old, Eric, the twelve-year-old, Jessica, the ten-year-old, and Myriam, the eight-year-old were already dreaming of their new home.

***

They awoke, all anxious to set foot into their new cottage. There was already some talk of who would have the bigger room, and which one was the most nicely decorated.

Breakfast was just around the corner, and the children were undergoing their morning routines. The smell of the cooking food made them hungry.

They hurried down to sit at the table, where Sophia was serving the food for her family.

As for Claude, he was still in his room, focusing on his thoughts, and plan of action, in order.

When the children came down to the dining room, Claude stepped out of his room to greet them.

They were happy to see their father, as they rushed over to give him a huge hug. Then, they all sat around the family table.

Claude joined his happy family as Sophia was finishing setting the table with the food that she had just cooked.

After the food was set upon the table, Claude told the children to eat well because the next meal would not be for at least six hours, as the trip would take them at least five.

It was a joyous atmosphere; everyone expected to see the gorgeous cottage described to them by their father.

Claude took the time to tell his children that they might have to deal with some unpleasant situations, but nothing worse than what they have already had to live with so far.

The kids were used to haunted places and already had a couple of close calls. However, they were prepared to face this new challenge.

After breakfast, it was time to pack. Sophia had already gathered the needed items to prepare a dinner for her family at their new house.

Claude performed some routine maintenance of the property, wondering about the unknown of what he and his dear family would be facing. Nothing seemed to terrify the children about ghost stories, and ghost realities, because they were born into this situation.

Claude was a vigilant, responsible father who would never endanger the lives of his beloved children. He was an expert on paranormal activity, and he was always aware of the potential risk, and danger, that his family was constantly facing. He was a fortunate father whose children were given a developed sense of awareness, as they were precocious.

The younger girl was so gifted that, on some occasions, she was the one to have found the last remaining mystery, or tragic event. Claude had certainly passed on his love for mysteries and adventure.

Sophia was a perfect match for Claude; he could not have asked for a better wife. The two parents were so bound together that there was not a single decision they did not make together.

As for the children, they were navigating in a pool of love and tenderness. Julian had a funny temperament. He always found some situations comedic; he was energetic and full of life. His younger brother, Eric, was more of an intellectual. He did not care too much for noise and turbulent situations. Eric liked to be left alone. He enjoyed walking in the woods, traveling, and studying.

Jessica, the oldest daughter, was a person whose likeable personality always helped her make a good impression. At school, Jessica was popular and well-liked, a perfect replica of her mother.

As for the baby girl of the family, Myriam, she was the one who possessed the gift of prediction. Myriam was born with a rare gift of clairvoyance, also a sensibility with the world of ghosts and spirits. She enjoyed every moment her when dad shared his latest experiences with her, and she loved to give her input on his approaches.

After ensuring that everyone had their seatbelts on, Claude slowly drove out of the driveway, and they were on their way. It would be five hours of suspense, and wonder, for the children, who already couldn't wait to be there.

Claude knew that he was driving his family to a wonderful little corner of paradise; he knew he'd live like a king once he chased away the ghost who was haunting this cottage.

***

"Look, Dad," said Julian. "It looks like there a private train travelling to this cottage."

Claude replied, "Well, that was not listed on the realtor's sheet. I will ask the realtor if, indeed, this is a private train belonging to the cottage."

"If this train belongs to the cottage, I want to learn how to drive it because I want to be the solo driver of it."

This provoked quick responses from his other brother, and sister, who argued for their fair share about who would drive it.

Claude had a good laugh and replied, "Julian may drive it. The rest of you will have to wait until you're older."

To this, Eric countered back saying "Dad, I am twelve, just a couple years younger. How long do I have to wait?"

"Well, no one needs to worry about it until I find out if the train belongs to the cottage."

It was almost 12:00, and the children had nothing to eat since their breakfast that morning. Obviously, they were getting cranky.

Claude told them to look out for the next restaurant and they would stop there and eat.

It did not take long for one of the children to call out and, in no time, they arrived at the restaurant and found a table.

They enjoyed their meal in silence, muted by their hunger.

After paying the bill, the conversation fell to the cottage, and some of the customers in the restaurant overheard the conversation. One of the men approached Claude and politely asked him, "Are you the new owner of the cottage? I'm from the area, and we heard it was sold."

"Yes," replied Claude. "My family and I are the new owners of the cottage. I suppose you have heard a lot of stories about this place. By the way, this is my wife, Sophia."

The stranger man shook Sophia's hand and introduced himself as Peter, then said in a low voice, "Don't you know this place is haunted by an evil spirit, or a ghost?"

"Yes," replied Claude. "I am aware. Just to let you know, I am an expert in that domain, and my family are used to these sorts of situation."

The man replied, "Whatever you do, be vigilant. I've never set foot into the cottage, but I surely have heard a lot of strange things coming from it. If I were you, I would be careful."

He asked Peter if he knew to whom the train that they saw earlier belonged.

"Sure, I do. It belongs to the cottage. Somehow, it has private drivers and crew. Now, I've never seen anyone of the crew I, but they have their own station, too."

"That sounds interesting," said Claude, making a note to find out more about who ran the train and how it came to be a part of the cottage.

He exchanged a few more words with Peter, and just before taking off, Claude asked if he would be willing to give him his phone number. "Yes, I sure can. Here is my phone number. Call me anytime."

***

They arrived in town without incident, all excited to arrive at the cottage. The last stop of the town was observed by Claude and, for the first time, the whole family could glance at the newly purchase cottage.

"Oh, wow!" exclaimed all the children. "This is a paradise."

"Not so fast, children. Remember, we will have some difficulties before declaring this a paradise. I sense that we are just about to face a troubling time, about to unveil a sad event that took place in this cottage."

"Whatever it is, once we overcome this haunting of the cottage, we will be like kings among the whole village," said Eric.

Jessica also added that she would be the one to introduce, and take care of, the visitors dying to visit the *célèbre* cottage.

With that said, Claude ushered them to the doorstep of the cottage. He told his children to wait for him before wandering off too far into the house. He wanted to be present everywhere they decided to go.

After a brief walk around the mansion, the children decided to walk upstairs to see which room they wanted. The rooms were almost identical, without enough variation to prompt any argument for anyone to claim one room over another.

The day was going as planned. Nothing out of the ordinary came to spoil the family's first visit to the mansion.

Claude was a little at odds with the fact, but he was thankful that nothing was happening on their first day.

Sophia offered to stay in the mansion while Claude ventured out in the cottage. Claude agreed with Sophia and was soon on his way to explore all that the cottage had to offer. He had already walked the area a little with the realtor, but there was so much more to explore.

***

Not long after passing a nearby barn, Claude found a trail, so he and his children decided to follow it to see where it would lead them. It was to be a pleasant surprise because they found a boat shed. The children were exuberant.

"Let's see that boat," Claude said, unlocking the door. "It looks nicely taken care of."

As they stepped into the garage, Eric shouted out, "That means there is a lake on the cottage! By the size of the boat, it must be a good-sized lake."

"Yes," asserted Claude. "There must be a huge lake, or river, attached to the cottage, or somewhere nearby."

At that point, they were so excited that, for a moment, Claude totally forgot all about the dark side of the cottage.

"Well, children, I won't make you wait much longer. We will be moving here during the next couple of weeks. We will still be keeping the other property we have; I will make this cottage our primary residence so you all can enjoy the beauty we now possess."

Shortly after, they arrived at an electric dam. "What a beautiful lake!" exclaimed all the children. "We can't wait to take a ride on the boat."

Jessica was somewhat afraid of deep water; she was visibly not impressed by the size of the lake.

Myriam was alert and joyful. She had a taste for adventure but, for some reason, the lake spooked her.

Knowing his daughter's awareness, and sensitivity, he asked, "Do you feel in danger, or that someone wants to hurt you?"

Myriam replied, "No, Dad, I am safe, for now. I just feel that something went wrong here. This beautiful lake has a secret."

"If you ever feel threatened, let me know. We'll move away from the lake."

"Thanks, Dad," replied Myriam.

"I am afraid we are not out of the woods. This is an enormous property. I am convinced we will encounter some difficulties."

Claude kept a close eye on his family. Because of his livelihood, protecting the safety of his children was his priority.

Claude was eager to return to the mansion, as he was missing Sophia.

On their way back, they also made a quick visit to nearby shed. At first sight, it was nothing special, just the power source for the dam. But they also found boxes of old books stacked on top of each other.

Claude mused that one of the previous owners might have been a librarian.

***

After a good five hours of adventure, Claude's family were on their way to the mansion. The children were hungry, so it did not take too long to return to their new home sweet home.

Sophia was happy to see the happy crew back and served them a warm meal. She realized that her younger daughter was somber. Sophia went over to her side, and Myriam tried to appease her mother's anxiety. "I'm just a little tired," the child said.

Sophia asked if she wanted a little nap before they drove to the hotel. Myriam answered, "No, Mom, I'll be all right." It was nearing the time to say goodbye to their new home, for now.

After having ensured that the door was secure and locked up, Claude slowly drove away from the beautiful cottage.

Chapter 3
A Mysterious Lantern

As Claude was driving out, he looked in the rear-view mirror of the van and noticed a mysterious glowing lantern shape by the "library" next to the powerhouse. He double-checked to see if he was, in fact, seeing a light. Sure enough, it had the form of a lantern. He kept driving slowly off the premises.

During that time, Sophia was busy with the kids, listening to their adventures.

Julian was the first one to mention something about the nice kept boat they had found in a shed.

Then, Eric changed the subject to the lake which they discovered, then the stunning discovery of the powerhouse. They sure had many things to talk about to their mother about.

For Jessica, she was pleased about the size of her room.

Jessica had already chosen her room and was ready to ensure that no one would take it away from her.

Sophia was jubilant to see her children's enthusiasm about the cottage. She suddenly realized that her younger daughter was somber again. She asked Claude if anything out of the ordinary had happened to Myriam.

To that, Myriam replied, "I am just fine Mom; I guess I am tired."

***

They arrived at the hotel.

Just when Claude opened the door, he saw the realtor talking to the receptionist of the hotel. "Good timing," said Claude. "I will ask the realtor if he can have a little chat with me."

He wished his family goodnight and walked over to the realtor and said, "Hello."

After a warm handshake, both men moved into the small dining area of the hotel and sat at a table.

The realtor asked how the trip to the property had gone.

Without losing a second, Claude went straight to the reason why he wanted to meet the realtor. "I wanted to ask about the powerhouse. You didn't show it to me during the tour."

The realtor replied, "Many believe that the start of the problematic situation revolves around this powerhouse. I was afraid that, if I told you about this powerhouse, you would ask me why it's no longer used. There is much documentation that you could find in the archives of the town about this powerhouse. However, no specific clues, or guidance, are available."

"I understand your situation, but your duties as a realtor were to tell me everything about the cottage. I was a potential buyer back then and, now, I am the owner, and you came to find out that I am an expert in the domain of supernatural events taking place in haunted places."

The realtor replied, "Claude, I know you don't understand and have the whole picture yet. Once you do, I am sure you will understand why I hid the truth. I have only heard some of the rumors that came out of this surrounding powerhouse, and the adjacent building. Trust me, it was an honest mistake with best of intentions. I am sure you will be the one to uncover the curse cast upon it."

Claude replied, "Do you have any clue of what took place there?"

"Nothing firm," said the realtor. "What circulate are only rumors."

"Hmm... Do you know anything about the old sawmill just downhill from the powerhouse?" asked Claude.

"All I know is it's said that the saw mill is attached to the curse."

Claude's imagination was at its best, showing him the opportunities awaiting him in conquering such a challenging situation. Claude liked the fact that the property, itself, was to be found a treasure, perhaps maybe a clue directing him to the core of the problematic situation.

After a brief exchange, and a handshake, Claude walked away from the table to regroup with his family. Once back with them, it was time to say goodnight.

The full moon was brilliant that night, and there was not one cloud in the blue sky.

Sophia was pleased about her day.

As for the children, they were so tired that it did not take long for them to fall asleep.

***

In the morning, the sun woke the family, one by one.

Almost immediately, the phone rang, and Claude answered the call, "Hello, may I talk to Claude, please?"

"This is Claude; how I may help you?" he said.

"Claude this is the administrator of the hotel. I just received an envelope for you. It will be at the front desk for you to pick up."

The line went dead, and Claude thought it odd the hotel administrator had called him by his first name. That was unusual for the service industry.

The children wanted to go back to their new home. They were dying to investigate everything. Julian was curious about how the turbine was made, and how it worked. Eric was a more of an intellectual person, and he was curious to uncover what mystery the old books they found contained. He was hoping to find some interesting stories and, maybe, some history.

Jessica was focused on claiming the room that she'd picked for herself, and Myriam only was interested in the beautiful scenery. She was captivated by nature and loved to be left alone to unveil the mysteries that nature had to offer her.

Claude was preoccupied with finding the first clue that would lead him to the heart of the problem that the cottage was cursed with.

Sophia agreed with her husband to move the family into the cottage as quickly as possible. After all, it was not terribly far from where they had their current residence. After a good night of sleep, Claude and Sophia would ask their children to start packing up all their belongings.

That night, Claude went to bed with plans to meet the town mayor. He was determined to solve the mystery surrounding this paradise and put the nightmare to rest.

Chapter 4
Taking the First Step

Claude drove to the library with a lot of wild thoughts running through his mind. He was curious to see if any clues, or documents, could be found. He arrived at the library and walked toward the circulation desk.

The librarian did not have a clue that Claude was an expert in paranormal situations and asked him if there was anything that he was looking for.

"Yes," replied Claude. "I recently bought a cottage not terribly to far from the town; it's reported to be haunted by an evil spirit. My first thought was to come to see if they were testimonies left behind by prior owners."

"I see," replied the librarian. "I will be more than happy to guide you in your search."

"Wonderful. Since you are from the area, I am curious to know is you ever spent some time there."

"Yes," she replied. "I used to live there for a short time. I moved far away from that house a few years ago. It was the best decision I ever made. Though, I do miss the countryside."

"Wow," said Claude. "This is exactly what I needed to find on day one."

After a moment of reflection, Claude asked the librarian, "What made you move away? I had some interesting conversations with the realtor, and he never claimed there were specific problems near the mansion."

She nodded and led him down the aisles, purposely avoiding answering his question.

Claude noticed that this aisle looked like no one had touched a thing in on it in many years. He stumbled upon a couple of old books that were related to the property.

Browsing through them, he made some discoveries but kept quiet because he figured that it was too early to talk about it. Claude needed more time, and also evidence, to back up his findings. He also wanted to secure all key witnesses who were still living in the town.

There was a particular book, a medium volume treasure vault hiding among the mysteries and codes speculating the cure for the cursed cottage. As Claude went to reach for the book, he felt a wind, like someone was walking behind him.

"Hmm…." said Claude. "Let's see what this medium book has to offer me. It is obvious that this book provoked a mysterious reaction on the behalf of the receptionist." Claude picked it up and blew the dust off the cover. To his surprise, it was a book that contained a memoir from a previous owner of the mansion.

Excited by his discovery, Claude noticed that there were five chapters. He had the feeling that the mastermind behind the mansion tragedy was bold in his esteem and saw himself as very clever.

Claude knew, with the years of experience he had acquired over his career, that some of the perpetrators bank on the stupidity of others to keep their identities hidden.

The curse was clearly affecting the entire past of individuals involved without their consent. Claude searched for more information that he could find from the library. He was ready to spend as much of time as required to gather all clues and facts. It was time that someone like Claude stepped in to solve this case, once and for all.

It did not take long for him to have some doubts, and suspicions, about the comportment of the librarian toward his presence in the library. Claude was preoccupied with how to smuggle the book out so that he could read it and decode the mystery of his newly purchased mansion.

But he realized that the librarian was watching his every move, and he found that a little odd. Knowing that she was a former owner of the cottage was enough for Claude to be cautious with the exchange that he had with her.

Claude was a clever individual who possessed a rare gift toward suspicious, and challenging, situations.

Time was going by, and Claude concentrated on any new findings that he could possibly get his hands on. He gathered the few books that he had chosen and left the library to take a little rest. That was a calculated setup so that he could see the reaction of the librarian.

Sure enough, as soon as Claude stepped out of the library, he could see from the window that the librarian was walking the aisle where he had found the mysterious book.

Realising that Claude had taken the book with him, the librarian rushed back to her desk; she was waiting at the entrance to remind him about the rules and conditions while visiting the library.

As soon Claude stepped into the library coming back from his little break, the she reminded him that all books needed to be checked out at the circulation desk.

"Oh, I am extremely sorry for having walked out without signing out the book," said Claude. "I promise you; it won't happen again."

***

Sophia was on her way to the library with the children; she wanted to give her husband a quick lunch since she figured that Claude would be hungry.

She entered the library with her children and walked to the front desk and asked the librarian if she knew where Claude was.

"Yes, sure," she replied. "Claude is actually in the fourth aisle of the library."

"Can I bring him a little lunch? I figure he must be hungry," asked Sophia.

"Let me tell him that you are here. For your convenience, we have a little room in the library for visitors. Feel free to use it."

"Thank you so much for your offer. We will wait for Claude there," replied Sophia as the librarian began walking toward Claude to let him know that Sophia was waiting for him.

As she reached Claude, she noticed that the book was not to be seen. "Claude, your wife is waiting for you in the family room. She brought you something to eat."

"Tell her I will be right there," replied a cautious Claude. He was not sure if he could trust the librarian.

After making sure that she was not in his sight, Claude took the book that had provoked the strange reaction from the librarian and placed it onto another shelf in a totally new aisle.

After covering up all evidence, Claude was on his way to the family room to meet his wife and children.

After hugging his wife and his children, Claude sat down toward the window, where he could keep an eye on the bookshelves.

Sure enough, Claude noticed the librarian walking toward the aisle where he had found the famous book. Nervously, she was searching to see where she could locate it.

Claude announced to Sophia that he had made some major discoveries. After having spent some time with his children and wife, Claude excused himself and walked back to the aisle.

By that time, the librarian was back at her desk.

This time off with his family had been good for Claude; he was refreshed. He walked back to the aisle of the library to continue his discoveries while the librarian kept a close eye on him.

Sure, enough Claude made another discovery that was about the old train station on the property.

However, it was missing the main aspect as to why the train was left stationary for so many years, or why previous owner did nothing to make it go again.

Claude saw the name PETRONAS several times. Could this PETRONAS be the engineer of the train, or a co-owner? Perhaps he was one of the many former owners.

Claude was finishing up his excursion at the town library before he decided to glance at the other aisles, fearful that the evidence would disappear before he could come back again.

Sure enough, after he had inspected a couple more aisles, Claude found another piece of interest; this one was connected to the old powerhouse situated on the bottom of the cottage.

In that source, it was said that, once upon a time, the dam had split open all the way to the middle. *So, the dam has been in place less than eighty years,* thought Claude. *That is good to know.*

Also, in the document, they were talking about a catastrophic situation, but extraordinarily little detail was given. *That is what I was thinking,* thought Claude. *I was right on since the first day I stepped my feet upon the cottage. But what could be the sad event that took place? Was it a deadly situation, or something else strong enough to make the cottage uninhabitable?*

That conclusion was based on the conversation that he had previously with the realtor, and the one not too long ago with the librarian.

Little by little, Claude was starting to put the pieces of the puzzle together. "Yes," said Claude, inhaling. "How many more of these details are still lying on shelves of this library, left behind for me to be discovered? All I can do is take this case one day at the time. Patience is the golden rule to resolve strange cases like this."

***

During this time, Sophia was pleased to see that Myriam's bad experience at the library had been forgotten though, still, she was cautious about how it happened, and where it happened.

The children were having a blast running around the cottage, walking by the train station. They were waiting for their dad to return so that they could ask his permission to explore their new toy.

Julian could not wait much longer to run the train with all his siblings aboard. He was constantly talking about the day when he would be given the okay to drive it.

There were some points of interest for every one of the children, which provided them sweet dreams about how to succeed in their new adventures.

***

Back at the library, Claude was thrilled to have found some information about the turbine. As he glanced through it, he came across the old sawmill that was, at one time, running off the powerhouse.

Well, I have now the tangible proof that this powerhouse described in this booklet is related directly to the cottage, he thought.

Just one little detail got Claude's attention. Why was that information not with the rest of the town's historical aisle, where he had spent most of his day? Could it be that someone before him had tried to research the cottage? Or could it be just a mistake?

I will ask the receptionist if she knows of anyone before me trying to solve the mystery, Claude thought. He put the title aside with the rest of the few books that he picked up and continued his exploration.

After he spent some more time examining the remaining aisles of the library Claude, decided to call it a day.

He was on his way to check out the one book he had selected. Once again, he was at the front desk, talking to the librarian, who had asked him many questions.

Claude became suspicious because of his experience that he had acquired over years dealing with inexplicable situations. *Hmm....* thought Claude. *This is a person of interest. Why does she insist so much to be the keeper of the town library?*

Claude also noticed that she seemed to switch from one personality to another, seemingly without even her knowledge. The prime character of Claude's intrigue was the one with the two tones of voice. One tone of voice was a woman's voice but, when it was time to dig dipper into the mystery of the personality he was dealing with, a man's voice would emerge.

When he went to the circulation desk to check out the book, the librarian eyed Claude, and he could see that an internal struggle taking place. And, in the end, she was forced to be compliant and let him borrow the famous book.

Now, Claude was not sure if he was, in fact, really talking to a woman. Puzzled, he managed to keep his cool.

After checking out the book, Claude asked her if she was all right.

To that, she replied, "I believe you are too curious. Why do you have a doubt about my identity? Did someone mention something about me to you?"

"No, no not at all," replied Claude. "I am only curious because you seem almost afraid of my presence here."

"Absolutely not, not at all. I am not afraid of you. You are the first person who has demonstrated so much of vigilance about the abandoned cottage."

"Well," replied Claude "I am sure you have figured out exactly what I am after." Having said that, Claude walked out of the library without another word.

CHAPTER 5
PETRONAS

Claude stopped by the post office on the way home to retrieve today's mail. When he arrived at the cottage, Sophia was happy to see her husband, as were the children. They greeted their father, running into his arms.

Dinner was ready, and the aroma of Sophia's cooking enticed everyone over to the family table.

The conversation centered on family activities. Everyone had something to say. The boys, obviously, had entered the train and explored their new toy. As for the girls, they were more abstract in their interests, like the beauty, and charm, of nature.

Sophia was pleased to hear the good stories that her children were exchanging at the family table. Even Myriam was enthusiastic about telling how she had spent her day.

The night was approaching, and the children were tired from their long day settling into their new home.

Claude told Sophia that he had made some interesting progress into the curse that the cottage suffered as he laid down the book that he had retrieved from the town library.

Sophia was pleased that Claude had found some interesting information about what had happened, and who might have been the culprit behind the curse.

After dinner, the children gathered together and were looking forward having sweet dreams about their excursion into the mansion.

Since electricity was fairly new in the village, an oil lamp, and a candle holder, were their prime sources for light. It was a warm sensation to see these oil lamps and candles burning, giving a unique charm to the warm atmosphere.

Claude sat at the kitchen table while Sophia finished up the last task in the kitchen before calling it a day.

Sophia brought out a cup of lemonade for her husband as she sat next to him.

Claude kissed her then said, "You know, my dear, I will be victorious from this experience, and we will have a little paradise for years to come, and for our grandchildren to enjoy."

"Yes," replied Sophia. "This cottage is more than a paradise."

Claude replied, "While at the library, I had some interesting conversations with the librarian. It was almost as if she was a man undercover the guise of woman. It all started when I encountered this memoir about the prior owner. And did you notice the librarian looking at our daughter?"

"Yes, I saw that. This is what prompted me to not stay much longer at the library," replied Sophia. "Who knows if that woman, at least in appearance, is not part of the problem?"

"I hear what you are saying," replied Claude. "No one will be permitted to perform any bad thing to our children under my watch."

Shortly after the children were all sleeping, Claude returned to the family living room sat down at the family table, lighted only with an oil lamp. With the warm ambiance, Claude decided to begin reading the book he was dying to decode.

Sophia was getting her room set up for the night. After having done so, she rejoined her husband at the family table in the living room. "Well, my dear, I hope you won't stay up all night long at the table. I know that, if you start to read a book, chances are that you will not put it down so easily."

"No," replied Claude. "I am tired and do not plan to stay up much longer. I have other things to do besides reading this book, as you know."

"Yes, my dear," replied Sophia. "I was only teasing you. Everyone knows how hard it is to break your concentration when you are focused."

Claude opened the book to the table of contents and saw that there were only five chapters listed. Also, there was no author. Maybe it was part of the coverup by the perpetrators, to force the author of the book to hide his identity and give a title to his master work. Reading the chapter titles, Claude saw:

> *"Chapter One: Miscommunication*
> *Chapter Two: Adversities*
> *Chapter Three: Crime and Remorse*
> *Chapter Four: The Inevitable*
> *Chapter Five: The Culprit"*

"Well," said Claude. "Undeniably, this ex-owner had plenty of bad experience with the curse imposed onto this cottage. I have the feeling that we will have to be more cautious, and vigilant, while working on this case. What surprises me the most is why did no one before me found this treasure book hidden in the library?"

Claude was perplexed as he glanced at the first chapter. He did not want to start reading the book now, for fear that it would keep him up all night.

"'Chapter One: Miscommunication'," said Claude. "That gives me the idea that the curse that fell on the first owner of the cottage had something to do directly with it because of some kind of miscommunication."

"Maybe a divorce was the source of it all. Or, maybe, someone got murdered in the mansion. What else could it be?" said a wondering Sophia.

"I know our children were born and raised into special circumstances because of the work that you are doing," Sophia continued. This situation existing in this mansion makes me uncomfortable, I know that nothing bad had happened to our children before but, this time, I have a bad feeling," said the anxious mother.

Claude replied, "Rest assured, my dear Sophia, I will never let any harm be done to our children. However, I will not back down, and I will confront this perpetrator." He closed the book sat quiet for a moment then reached for his wife's hand.

Claude and Sophia walked to their room, and both fell asleep not too long after they had lain their heads onto their pillows. The night went well, as everything was peaceful for the family, who were all recuperating from a busy day.

***

In the morning, Claude got out of bed, feeling refreshed. He had a clearer idea about how to approach the curse imposed onto the cottage.

After breakfast, the happy family all pitched in to finish the last bit of moving into their new home.

Claude soon went into his newly designated study. During the time was at his desk, he had started to read the chapter one of the mysterious book; Claude simply could not put it down.

From time to time, he was taking notes on another piece of paper. He then stumbled upon a mysterious story about a doll. Absorbed with his reading, Claude avoided anything that could distract him from the content, and the tone, of the memoir.

While reading about the mysterious doll, Claude became very engrossed in the story. So much had happened. It was both sensational, and disastrous, at the same time.

The story about the mysterious doll is as follows: First, the doll was haunted and still hidden somewhere. Second, the doll was blindfolded; the reason for this was not mentioned. However, they said that serious consequences would follow if they found that someone had disobeyed, and the doll was not blindfolded. Third, this doll had mysterious powers to harm whoever it shall see.

"Well," said Claude. "I will inform my children about a possibility of finding a doll somewhere on the property and, if found, they would have to let it alone and have them tell me where it's located."

Sophia overheard Claude's last sentence and walked in room, asking, "My dear, what is this new find? I overheard you talking about a doll."

"Yes, I have just read about a mysterious doll that is the heart of the problem. However, it is not mentioned as the main source and cause but, according to my experience, something tells me it *is* part of the main problem."

Sophia replied, "If that is the case, then, make our children aware of the potential find, and warn them of the grave consequences of even lifting it up from its hidden place."

"That exactly my idea, Sophia. We will tell them to immediately come home to let one of us know of its location if they find this mysterious doll," replied Claude. "In the meantime, I know it would be hard for the girls to do so because, according to the story, it is a very pretty doll."

Sophia was preoccupied with the thought that one of her girls could fall victim to the cursed object. Internally, she began to panic. Perhaps Myriam already was under the scope of the perpetrator.

Sophia, after having shared her concern, waited for a few minutes. Then, she decided to embark upon her duties in the kitchen.

Meanwhile, Claude had started to read the second chapter, which mentioned a lady who used to live in town but disappeared after a horrible crime was committed not too far from the powerhouse.

***

The former owner recalled that the lady suffered from mental illness. One day, she wrote the former owner, telling him that she was seeking vengeance to get even with her enemy who had wished upon her bad luck. She had a doll that she made many years ago.

On that day, she decided that the doll was part of the plot against her. She reflected, every day, that she had told the doll everything she did and everywhere she went.

"The doll had to go," said the lady. "I cannot endure one more minute of her presence, and I shall execute my disposal right now."

But, before she disposed of the doll, the lady did something that no one expected. She decided to render a visit to a witchcraft master to ask him to put a curse upon the doll to punish it.

As she arrived at the house, the lady took one long and last look at the beautiful doll and gave her a final hug.

Shortly after having disposed of the beautiful doll on the desk, the witchcraft person introduced himself as PETRONAS and asked the lady, "Are you sure you want to do this?"

"Yes," replied the sick lady. "This doll has betrayed me in many ways and, now, it is time for the doll to be held accountable for the misfortune that I encounter in my personal life."

"I will do this for you, if you absolutely want it, but I have to be relieved from any bad aftermath that this doll will be responsible for," said the annoyed witchcraft performer.

"How much this will cost me?" asked the sick lady. "Anything you want, I am ready to give it all, if I have to."

"What kind of curse do you want?"

"Ensure that the doll would create lots of confusion, and disasters."

"Okay. I will curse this beauty, but I will also warn anyone who will encounter it. And as for you, my dear lady, if you try to break these rules, you will die instantly. Now, do you accept these conditions?"

"Why should I be exposed to such a demand?" asked the obviously aggravated lady.

"Because you will die one day, and your beautiful doll will always be a source of attraction long after your departure."

"Whatever the cost, I am ready to pay the full amount."

PETRONAS nodded and performed the terrible curse. The performer took a grave look at the lady. Then, PETRONAS took a piece of cloth and wrapped it around the eyes of the beautiful doll. Solemnly, the performer declared that the blindfold should never be removed.

Immediately upon covering the beautiful doll, a movement was felt in the air, and the curse was laid.

And, for the sick woman's audacity, he used his power of clairvoyance to tell her, "You will commit a horrible crime in the cottage where you will lay down the doll. This crime will cost your freedom. You will never be brought to justice, but your freedom will be stolen from you while finding refuge in a convent.

"You will be long gone before this memoir will be read…. And I will also be long gone, but my skeleton will be all over the place and, if challenged, I shall have to come back to render justice.

"You oversee disposing of the doll wherever you want. There will come a time when the chosen one will uncover the eyes of the doll."

With this curse imposed onto her favorite doll, and having paid the witchcraft performer, the lady walked out the building; she went for a cup of coffee.

After she enjoyed her fresh cup, the lady walked toward the cottage and disposed of her doll by throwing it near the powerhouse. Nervously, she ran away from the scene and went to her daily occupation.

***

Claude finished the last paragraph. "My goodness," he said. "I am amazed no one before me read this masterly piece of evidence. Everything is well-described."

Sophia asked her husband, "Why this book is so important?"

Claude replied, "I believe I have found the key of the misery imposed onto this cottage. However, this chapter is still missing some important facts. Maybe the following chapter will tell me more about the clandestine rendezvous of the sick women."

Sophia offered a cup of coffee to Claude and went back to her duties while he turned the page to reveal the next chapter.

Chapter 6
Crime

Claude let Sophia know that he was studying intensely and preferred to not be disturbed until he finished the book.

Before delving into the next chapter, Claude took a well-deserved break so he could relax; that helped him to classify the information that he had already retrieved.

"I guess it's time for me to go back to work," said Claude. "I just can't wait to see what happened to this sick lady, and how far she executed her evil plan."

With anticipation, Claude re-opened the booklet to continue finding out the rest of the suspenseful story from the memoir of a former owner.

That next chapter was longer than the others, so much detail, and clarification, was provided. In fact, that chapter revealed what had happened to the crazy lady after she disposed of her now dangerous doll.

One of the former owners who knew the crazy lady recalled, in detail, her role and what took place at the cottage.

***

One afternoon, the lady was watering her plants in the garden.

After having made a couple trips to the well, she emptied the watering can and went inside her home to have a cup of coffee.

Once she finished her refreshment, she went back to the garden and, to her surprise, she found four big rocks glued to the bottom of her watering can.

Frustrated, she looked around to see if she could find the culprit. She took that innocent prank so seriously that she was losing her mind over something so simple. Could it be that her reaction was provoked by the spell caster?

She became paranoid that someone had followed her while she was visiting the spell caster and, now, that individual sought to get her.

After having looked vigilantly, and seen nothing abnormal, she decided to pull the rocks out of her watering can.

Though she struggled, she succeeded in removing the rocks and continued her project. But she was obviously upset and wanted to get to the bottom of the suspicious trick that someone had pulled on her.

Since she lived next to the cottage, she had her suspicions about what could have been taking place, and who was the culprit behind this nasty set up was.

For the rest of the day, she presumed that the children of the cottage owner were to blame, so the crazy lady was out for vengeance. She understood neither the parents, nor the children, liked her.

That night, she had nightmare after nightmare. It was 2:00 in the morning, and she still had not had any proper sleep. Now, she was starting to pay dearly for her adventure with witchcraft.

***

The morning arrived, and the crazy lady was feeling more disgusted; all she wanted was vengeance.

She soon arrived at the town restaurant. Sure enough, the owner of the cottage was sat at the table with his family.

What good timing thought the crazy lady. *All I must do is find a place not too far from them.* She went and sat at the table near the family.

Soon, a waitress came over to ask her if she wanted a cup of coffee and presented her the menu of the day.

"I'll take some coffee. Give me time to order my meal."

"Fine," replied the waitress. "I will come back to take your order."

The family occupying the cottage were not pleased to see their weird neighbor at the restaurant that morning.

A frustrated Romeo said, "Dad, you know I am tired of this lady. Can we just move somewhere else?"

The crazy lady overheard Romeo.

Luke, the father, saw the reaction of the crazy lady and replied, "Romeo, I know you are tired of seeing her around. Let me assure you, I will not let this lady do you any harm."

The crazy lady was visibly enraged by the answer that Luke had given his son. Wild thoughts began running through her mind. She wanted so badly to find who had glued the rocks to her watering can.

To add even more to her madness, the fact that the other members of the family of five had agreed with Luke's response.

Noam, Luke's older son said, "Yesterday, I had a good time playing with this ugly lady."

The crazy lady's ear went straight up, like a freshly sharpened knife, as she was grasping to hear every word Noam had to say. "I glued four rocks on the bottom of her watering can."

Everyone had a good laugh, except for the crazy lady, who was out for vengeance.

After they had finished eating and paid for their breakfast, Luke and his family stepped out of the restaurant. No one had even an inking of the idea about the evil plan that the crazy lady was grooming in her mind. "An eye for an eye, and a dead for an insult," the lady said in a hushed tone.

She then went to the town store, bought a suit with a pair a shoe, then started on her way home. But, before getting home, she made an appointment at a beauty shop for the early morning. She then put a final touch to her devilish plan.

Yes, she thought. *I will put poison into this drink, and I will make it a pink color, knowing that this color is more attractive.*

I will pretend to be an agent from a nearby company and will serve this drink to Luke while he is busy, and thirsty, from operating his sawmill. I will put enough poison to see him die from a nearby location.

She was about to go home when she was confronted by PETRONAS while coming out of the restaurant. She stopped, scared that he was there to thwart her brilliant plan.

But, merely taking her aside, the master of deception said to her, "Woman, the convent you will go to is well-hidden. No law enforcement will find you. It is part of a remote wooded area of this town. As a matter of fact, the train could take you there."

"Are you referring to the train that I have hidden so well? The key no one came close to find for all these years?" asked the lady.

"In that case, your masterly plan will not work because I will never divulge to anyone where I laid it. As a matter of fact, you just gave me a brilliant idea. Let us see, what about if I make this key disappear once and for all, then, what will you do?" asked the triumphant lady.

"Let us see, I am witnessing one side of your hidden personality that, so far, I wasn't able to discover, even thanks to my clairvoyance and knowledge. I now know this hidden side.

"Don't even bother to mess with the key. Let me tell you, in advance, that this would not do you any good. As a matter of fact, it will serve only to make your living unbearable. Do yourself this favor and turn in the key before I take it by force!"

The lady reflected upon the last sentence of her unwanted guest then said, "All right, master, I will voluntarily give you the key in return of such of loyal act. What could you do to render the remainder of my sentence less miserable?"

Jubilant at his success, the unwanted guest replied, "Do not worry about this; I will arrange things so that you will be considered a gifted person. I like music so, with the power I have been given, I will make you the director of the holy hymns for the convent. You will do such of wonderful job that no one will even suspect that you are mentally ill. And, soon, you will be vested with power. From time to time, I will come back to see you under different disguises. Rest assured; it will be me. You will have to keep this secret, as I will be spying on you and all your activities.

"I want to make this convent discovered because of its multiple wonderful possibilities to render the town a little bit more prosperous, and suitable to the majority of the residents."

"I see, you will be using me as your personal shield, and door, opener to possibly ruin the holy life of the nuns living there," replied the lady. "I see how evil you are."

"No, absolutely not; I do not want to destroy the life of those nuns. My goal is to prepare them for modernization," he replied. "I want the whole town to realize the beautiful potential that this area has to offer to enrich the growing population of this town.

"You are trying to misjudge my intentions; let me tell you that you do not have even a small idea. I want to bring a revolution to this lovely place.

"The convent is adjunctive to the growing town. The unknown surroundings of the convent could be used to upkeep it. This would also create potential new vocations for the nuns residing in the convent. I have prayed, long ago, that my eyes would see this wonderful opportunity.

"This would benefit both of us, the convent, and the whole town because they are given the opportunity to discover the richness of the land that the convent possesses." Now that the expert in had his target surrender peacefully, he was already making plans to modernize the convent.

It was like a dream come true. But, for now, it was primordial for the master to work under cover especially now that the projected target had voluntary accepted his offer.

"Now, lady, let us go back to the main subject that was the train. I know we have walked away from the conversation. Now, it is time to look again and finish our business."

"The train," articulated the poor lady. "Why do you have much of interest into this vapor monster? I know it will make no difference soon, if you have the key, or you do not. So, I will provide you with it. I have only one request before providing you the key. Keep the provider name incognito."

"Yes, I will be keeping your identity secret; you do not have to worry about this. I have other plans lined up; everything will fall into place."

"I am curious to find out what you know about this famous train so much that you had to bring the subject back to the table," said the lady.

"As you know, this train was the proud product of an engineer who built it working long-hour days, in and out, to provide his family with luxury transportation.

"Also, this individual had a dream, and a bright future in front of him, and his family, until the day I intervened to reverse the progress he was achieving.

"I look out to every little detail to work for my advantage. It is very well-calculated and masterly built together hat, tone day, I saw that my masterly project had been infiltrated by the wise man.

"Things weren't going the way I wanted them to. I became envious of the knowledge, and perseverance, of the father of four children. He was a calm and reflective person, the exact opposite of you."

The lady was listening, focusing intently on every sentence from her interlocutor's mouth, busy gathering information that confirmed what she had already known about the train.

However, she never did hear it from the source. The mastermind con-artist had hypnotized her, and her ears were glued to the lips of her lecturer, an enthusiastic interlocutor, whose interest was to groom his victim, was pleased to realize that the lady was absorbing the half truth about the hidden dark story of the train.

With anticipation, he continued where he left off about the telling believable story of the town train.

"As you may know, this train was the source of a thousand investigations. Many engineers had come to try fix this wonder. No one was successful and, up to today, while the train has been abandoned, the town consider it lost in revenues.

"I know the reason why you took the key out of this machine and, let me tell you, it is not necessary; all the truth when you say it is because of the loud horn of the train.

"You still resent the day, many years from now, when one of your family members many will be found dead, like they were glued on the seat. That is the reason why, today, that you need to rectify an innocent situation in your mind, made to remind you of your family tragedy."

The crazy lady was grooming the idea of getting even with her neighbor for the prank that one of his sons had played on her. He was banking upon the craziness of the lady, which would set the chain of events into motion.

***

"Interesting," said Claude. He could not take his eyes off the book. "I am curious to find out what happened to the train. Though I now understand why the librarian was so nervous, and reluctant, to let go of this book."

"I suspect this person had a direct part to play into this whole ordeal," said Sophia. "The first time I saw this person, something told me to be careful."

"Yes," replied Claude. "How are the children doing? Are they respecting our rules and expectations?"

"Yes," replied Sophia. "As a matter of fact, here they are, coming into the mansion."

Claude went to see his children and interact with them, asking them how they liked the place so far.

An explosion of happiness came out of them all; they were excited to ask when they would take a deeper walk with their parents onto their property.

"Very soon," said Claude. "I have to finish reading an important piece of information and, then, I am all yours. Do me a favor and stay together while walking."

"Yes, Dad, we will," replied the children. With that, they went into the kitchen to grab some lunch that their mother had prepared for them.

Shortly after having eaten, the children stepped out of the mansion and went back to their little hide and seek game.

Sophia was keeping a close eye upon the property, well aware that they weren't safe until her husband put to rest the curse imposed onto the lovely cottage.

As for Claude, he walked back to his room to continue his reading about the circumstance involving his newly acquired domain.

Claude sat at his desk and reopened the book and was preparing to finish the entire chapter. He looked around his room and noticed that he had forgotten to close his door.

After having closed the door, he then began to read in the quiet atmosphere to learn about the rest of the dilemma that he had to confront.

Sure enough, as soon he started to read the chapter, his attention was, once again, taken by the precision and mysterious fashion, and style, of the words.

PETRONAS was talking about multiple reasons why the train was left stationary for so long. Claude avidly read the continuation of the mysteries surrounding the history of this famous train. He was now reading the part where PETRONAS had received the key from the crazy lady.

***

"I must thank you so very much, dear lady, for having conserved this key and not have lost sight of it. Without this your desire for vengeance strongly guiding you, this moment would not had happened.

"Now, I know that you are afraid. I will devolve the rest of the story. I want to reassure you that I will keep my word. I promised you that I will never reveal your name while you are still alive.

"Yes, you will be quite well-protected in the convent after having lived a 'holy life' and having brought modernisation to the convent."

The crazy lady was premediating on how to teach a severe lesson to the irresponsible father.

"Oh, yes! I almost forgot a detail," PETRONAS said. "It is about the twelve-year-old boy who will die on the train."

The lady jumped off her seat. That was the last thing she wanted to hear from PETRONAS. "Why do you have to bring this boy into our conversation? There is not a day that goes by that I do not think about him, and his fate.

"I know that I had my guilty share playing into his mysterious death. After all, he was as naughty as the one who had glued four rocks to the bottom of my garden watering can."

PETRONAS replied, "His spirit still haunts the train, and the nearby buildings. He resembles a lost soul looking for his mate. He has extremely limited capacities. You took the life of this young man and deprived him of future."

The lady felt like she was nailed to the wall, having no place to go. "Wow," she said as she was quietly thinking about restitution, and fair due, for her involvement in the crime.

"I know that the boy in question became a target of your evil simply because you had judged that he did not like you. You concluded that his goals were motivated by his dislike of you."

The agitated lady replied, "He got what was coming to him. If you play with fire, you get burned.

If you are trying to make me feel bad about his passing away, I must say to you, get yourself together and go on with your miserable life."

Imperatively PETRONAS added, "Lady, let me tell you, your favorite doll is taken over by the boy who was murdered. He is using your lovely doll.

"Now, I am revealing to you the deepest secret about my cast upon your favorite doll. I shall return also as the librarian when time is right. Rest assured, before that event will occur, you and I will have long since passed away."

The surprised lady asked, "Didn't I just agree to be yours in this life? I do not recall signing away my afterlife as well."

PETRONAS replied, "I know this may come to a surprise to you, but there is absolutely nothing you could do to change, or reverse, the chain of events. The whole ordeal will come to ending when your favorite doll is freed from the curse imposed on it.

"The chosen one at the time of this critical moment will have to follow the instructions given to the lucky owner in order to finalize the removal of the curse. For now, my dear possession, I shall let you go."

"May I ask you," the lady began, "Where this instruction could be found? I, myself, know that I did everything in my power to neutralize any means, or talent, to come and destroy the curse that I voluntary accepted to cast on it."

PETRONAS replied, "This detail, for now, must remain secret. I must go back to my duties. As you know, I am a busy man, and I have lots of requests every day. None come close to your evil, rest assured. I will be on time with all my predictions, and you will also be on target with all the specific time allowed for my success."

With that said, PETRONAS left her standing near the door.

As for the poor lady, she was left speechless, as her mind thought of multiple questions. She was happy to see her unwanted visitor finally leave.

Finishing up her cup of coffee, she soon was on her way out, rage and deception guiding her motions and thoughts.

The crazy lady reached into her pocket and retrieved a little piece of paper, a reminder of what she planned to do to seek vengeance for the innocent joke played on her by the neighbor boy. She disliked her neighbor so much that she was planning a severe, and unjust, restitution.

It was a gray afternoon. The sun was covered by thick clouds, and the atmosphere was perfect for a storm to develop at any time. The gray sky had a negative impact on the mood of the crazy lady.

***

She reached her home and sat at her kitchen table, deep in concentration. In the quiet of the room, she was thinking about what her unwanted guest had told her at the restaurant. She was so blinded by vengeance that she did not see her immediate thoughts were fulfilling PETRONAS's prediction.

Pleased with every little detail of her plan for vengeance, the crazy lady grabbed a piece of paper and began to take notes, ensuring that none of the small details would be disregarded. She had come up with a plan perfectly orchestrated to ensure that Luke would not be found, at least for a couple of days, even months, after her vengeance was executed.

That night, she went to bed early, as Luke was on his way home after a hard day at the family sawmill. Luke had no idea of his neighbor's evil intention.

Luke could not sleep well. He was preoccupied with the thought that his neighbor would come to cause harm to his family. He confided in his wife, "Since Noam played an innocent prank on the lady, she has become so hateful. Her whole attitude shows; she is extremely consumed."

"Yes," replied Danielle. "I've noticed this, myself. What really makes me suspicious was witnessing her behavior earlier this morning at the town restaurant."

Luke paused for a while then said, "My dear Danielle, all we can do is continue doing what we've been doing for many years. This means to keep a close eye on her and restrict our children from encountering this undesirable individual."

"Yes," replied Danielle. "This task is becoming a little harder. As our children age, we, as parents, don't necessary know as much about what they are doing."

"Dear, we all have been through this phase of life. Let me tell you, I know that our children love beyond any doubts that we ever could. I am confident we will be able to continue living in this little corner of paradise."

After having said that, Luke blew out the candle, and the room felt into the darkness of the night, which made for the perfect ambiance to allow Luke and Danielle to finally fall asleep again.

That night, Luke had was plagued with recurring nightmares. During one of them, he was under attack by some monsters set out to kill him. However, he succeeded in ensnaring them. During their captivity, he learned that they had received their mission, and orders, from the crazy lady.

The nightmare made Luke jump out of the bed which, in turn, caused Danielle to wake. "What's the matter with you?" she asked.

"Oh, dear," replied Luke. "I just had a nightmare that concerned me and our undesirable neighbor."

Danielle replied, "Thank goodness it was only a nightmare. Now, let us go back to sleep; we will talk about this in the morning."

After the strange nightmares, Luke went back to sleep and, this time, he was not affected by any nightmare.

***

The morning arrived without any further incident, so Danielle was confident that everything would be all right.

The crazy lady was putting the finishing touch on her evil plan when she noticed that Luke was on his way to the family sawmill building. *Perfect*, she thought. It was a hot and humid day, just what she needed in order to enact her revenge.

The crazy lady went over to the icebox and put in the lemonade she had just made; she needed to give it time to cool.

Luke had been working diligently for a few hours now. The crazy lady put her lemonade in two different bottles, one was the real and the other one the poisonous drink. She labeled the poisonous bottle as, *"This will give you a wonderful day!"*

The crazy lady went to the village store to pick up her disguise, then walked home.

After having dressed herself to cover her real identity, she walked down to offer some refreshment to Luke at work.

She soon arrived at Luke's sawmill and had a brief conversation with him. The crazy lady told Luke that she was a vendor for the town during the summer, and she was making random checks to see if anyone in town was thirsty.

The crazy lady was so well disguised that Luke did not even recognize her; he was taken off guard because it was the first time that he saw her.

The crazy lady took the bottle out of her bag, ensuring that Luke received the one she had labeled as *"This will give you a wonderful day!"*

Luke smiled as he read it.

The crazy lady poured some lemonade into a cup and presented it to Luke.

It was a splendid afternoon. There were no clouds, and the sky was perfectly blue. Luke started to drink his lemonade.

Not too long after taking his first sip, Luke started to feel strange. Since he had already swallowed some of the poisonous drink, it was too late. He spit out the remainder of his lemonade but fainted soon. LAs was planned by the evil crazy lady, he fell into the agitated river.

"There you are my friend. An eye for an eye, and a death for a prank played. This is how I deal with any individual who dares to prank me, or mess with my belongings."

Nervously, but professionally, the crazy lady got up, picked up the rest of the lemonade and her cups, and walked back home before any member of Luke's family came to check on him.

***

She just arrived home just in time to witness Danielle going down to see how her husband was doing. Everything was running smoothly.

***

Like usual, Danielle called his name, but she received no response. She tried again; this time louder. Still nothing, Luke was nowhere to be seen.

Danielle decided to walk to the building to see if he was busy working on the machinery but, still, Luke was nowhere to be found. Danielle could sense that something was wrong. It was not like her husband to just simply disappear without any trace.

Danielle ran to the mansion regroup all her children and tell them to stay indoors. The concerned wife had not seen her husband since breakfast. It did not take long for the children to realize what was going on; some of them already were in tears.

"We are not staying one more night in this place!" said Danielle. "Let us go to a motel in town. I will call the police to have them investigate to where my husband could have disappeared to."

Leaving everything behind, Danielle was on her way to town at the search of a motel.

***

During that time, the crazy lady savoured her victory. She set aside her makeup and outfit then put the dress into the wooden stove, destroying any evidence that was pointing at her. She then sat at her kitchen table. To her surprise, PETRONAS was standing in the doorway.

"Where are you coming from, and what do you want?"

PETRONAS replied, "Dear, it is time for you to say goodbye to this beautiful town and enter into your predicted holy place. You do not have a minute to think about it, you are already condemned; your evil action is crying for vengeance. You don't have for much longer; you have to leave behind everything you own and follow me."

The crazy lady was annoyed. "I just can't leave here right now. Don't you think it will look suspicious if I go now and follow your order?"

"Lady, you do not have any time to waste. Your vocation is calling you."

As PETRONAS said this, the crazy lady saw a policeman making his way over to the property to investigate the mysterious disappearance of Luke.

Not terribly long after the departure of the crazy lady, an intense investigation was conducted. That was not the first time the cottage was the location of a vicious crime.

***

During that time, Danielle was with her children at the town hotel, arranging the last detail in order to leave the beautiful town once and for all.

***

That was the end of the chapter. Claude thought that, maybe, the one who had written the book was

Danielle, like it was her own personal journal but, at the last minute, she decided to leave behind her memoir to warn other.

"Did they ever find Luke?" asked a curious Claude. "Now, I am starting to get the picture: the mother moved out of the mansion with her family and, then, the cottage was put up for sale for another time."

Claude decided to start reading the next chapter, inevitably piqued by his own curiosity to see if any clues were to be given to the whereabouts of Luke.

The chapter then took an interesting turn. Instead of reading if Luke had been found, Claude was discovering what happened with the crazy lady and PETRONAS.

"This is worth a read," said Claude. "The mystery of this beautiful cottage will be, once and for all, put to rest, and the whole town will be able to enjoy, once again, this beautiful wonder." After drinking a fresh cup of coffee, Claude continued his reading.

***

Right after the murder of Luke, PETRONAS was at the lady's house with imperative order to follow him to her next destination.

The crazy lady knew that she could refuse, guided by fear, but she thought better of it, knowing that PETRONAS would have his way. Before getting to the last part of the road, PETRONAS stopped by a beautiful secret garden on the way.

No one had known about the garden because PETRONAS had made a mysterious entry which no one could find at first. It was a beautiful garden full of trees, flowers, and birds flying around. The peace and serenity of the garden was pure, and enviable, as the atmosphere was refreshing for anyone who could enter its wonder.

"Wow!" exclaimed the crazy lady. "This would be worth my craziness to be able to die in a paradise like this. After all, it would help me to become even more than holy while forced to live as a nun in a reclusive convent."

PETRONAS was not pleased with her last statement. He replied, "Hold on, lady. Because of your need for vengeance, I have lost control over this garden. Rest assured, no one will be able to find this secret gate until the day the lucky person succeeds unlocking this chapter."

***

Claude now knew that there was a secret garden adjoined, somewhere, to his property, possibly hidden over time. It would be difficult for the new owner to maintain it all, possibly because of dead branches and leaves.

"Interesting," said Claude. "And I am the lucky owner of this mysterious hidden gate of this garden with an unknown location. I am dying to continue reading to see if I can find out any more details."

Chapter 7
Appearance of the Doll

Now, Claude had a clearer picture of the indemnities of the crazy lady and reason why she never was arrested or put on trial. It seemed that she had only appeared while someone occupied the mansion. Other than that, she remained unseen.

Claude was reading the book without the knowledge that he was on the path of enacting a tragic event remarkably like his reading and discovery. As a matter of fact, Claude and his family were already on the radar of the bizarre circumstance.

Claude was captivated by how the writer was able to keep him in suspense, forcing him to read more chapters after chapter. Finally, after having his last drop of coffee, Claude resumed his reading, anticipating more evidence, and clues.

***

The crazy lady now was furious and out in the open. No one was around, and she was all out for vengeance. She thought, *If I succeed to catch PETRONAS off guard, it means the end of my dilemma.* Because the crazy lady had a corporal appearance but, in fact, was a fictional person; PETRONAS was always one step ahead of her.

"I suppose your clairvoyance has unveiled my real identities to your sense of rare scrutiny," replied the lady. "Now, if I am fictional, how could I have a 'holy death' in a convent surrounded by nuns?"

PETRONAS reflected for a moment then replied to his guest, "Don't you worry about what is fact versus fiction. Your whole life has been nothing but a big lie. I have been following you for a while now.

"I concluded that not only were you fictitious, but a deceptive illusion. However, having said this, you have caused irreparable damage, where lives of the innocent had been taken away by deception."

The lady replied, "Now, I suppose you were playing hide and seek, all along, until the day you came to have enough with your secretive game and the factor of time had connected you to talk with me.

"All the time, you are interested in me, and my activities. This should have been a warning sign, but I neglected this little detail. I am amazed I was able to fool a whole town, plus a different owner, while you were aware of the scam that my presence in this town truly is."

"Your dishonesty, lady, is beyond anything I can imagine but, wait, necessary because of the role given to you to put at rest this curse imposed on the cottage," replied the victorious PETRONAS.

Now, the crazy lady was pinned to the wall by her strange master, who sat in a garden, where only one designed individual was permitted entry. "I suppose you are talking also about yourself, PETRONAS. You really think you know everything. I also know a dirty secret of yours," replied the lady.

That last sentence made PETRONAS uncomfortable. However, he managed to regain control over his senses, and the tense situation. "The garden you see in is a real piece of land belonging to the cottage, just as you are truly talking to me. No one came to find it because of the mysterious, invisible gateway I had to create to protect my craft from being destroyed. Just stop and think for a minute, if you had found that gate, what would you have done?"

After a moment of reflection, PETRONAS continued, "Although you are fiction, that doll of yours is real, and you have created a lamentable situation where several families felt victimized because of its real presence."

The surprised lady replied, "Sir, why do you refer to my lovable doll as soon you see the perfect opportunity?"

He replied, "Because you are the soul of this creation, although, the little boy who really died because of your evil is using this beautiful doll as a vehicle until he will be free and laid to rest."

"Oh, no, do not tell me you are breaking our agreement!" said the furious lady. "Didn't we agree I would become your servant, and you would grant me all my wishes?"

"Yes," replied PETRONAS. "However, our agreement sustains only the fictious character you impersonate. You did not mention anything while signing the accord about you being aware of all that you do, even after your treachery of passing away."

The lady replied, "How clever on your part. I see that you have weighed all the pros and the cons of our agreement; how could I have missed this?"

PETRONAS replied, "That is simple, my dear. In a moment of blind vengeance, your clairvoyance had been duped, and you were not totally in control of your actions. Besides, the truth always comes to the surface while lies are always are bound to be found and defeated."

"Are you talking about yourself? Remember, you are just as fictional as I," replied the lady.

PETRONAS replied, "I do realize that I am also a fraud. However, my role in this whole ordeal is not only to be evil, but to impersonate a trusted, relatable individual. My profession demands a lot more of a sophisticated manner to enable me to render the service I offer to my client."

The crazy lady gave a disdainful look to PETRONAS and replied, "Now I see the plenitude of your exterior appearance, versus the monster you constantly guard and protect. I must remind you that, one day, you will be also in the same predicament that I am in today, without my consent; must I remind you of this?"

***

During Claude's reading, something took place. Myriam had spotted the doll and alerted her brothers and sister. "Look over there. Look at this beautiful doll!" exclaimed Myriam as she pointed at it.

"Wait," replied Jessica. "Is this the doll Dad talked to us about? Looks very well like it is. This is the doll we have been warned to let our parents know about. Can you see that her eyes are blindfolded?"

Everyone attention was directed toward Myriam's new discovery but, before Myriam took another step forward, the doll had vanished.

The children were excited, running toward their new family home. "Mom, Dad!" They all exclaimed in unison. "We just saw the famous doll. All we know is that it appeared briefly and then vanished almost right away."

Claude was still in his room, reading the book. He had the door of his room cracked open, and he heard his children's excitement. He rushed out of the room, fast as lightning, and then stepped into the kitchen, where the children were still fired up from their experience.

"Well, children, take me to where you spotted this doll," said Claude, nervously.

The children were on their way to show the exact place where they had found the infamous doll.

"Here, Dad, this is where we saw the doll. I was the first one who noticed its presence," said Myriam as she walked toward the direction where the doll made its first mysterious appearance.

Claude replied to Myriam, "Be careful. I know you are prompt, and agile. Whatever you do, do not even touch this doll. It looks like it has a mind of its own," said Claude.

Eric said, "Look, Dad, the grass even has changed color. The doll has some mysterious power to be able to change it."

While Claude was with the children, investigating the new event, Sophia left the kitchen and rejoined the rest of her family. She noticed that her husband was taken off guard and struggled with the discovery made by their children. Walking over to his side, Sophia asked Claude, "What is the issue?"

"My dear Sophia, something is not right with this picture," replied Claude. "Do you remember, while at the town library, Myriam felt sick for a brief moment?"

"Oh, yes," replied the anxious mother. "Do you mean that Myriam is in an evident danger, or felt like a victim of a spell?"

"I don't really know," replied Claude. "This is too early to determine. I am very anxious about the scenario."

Suddenly, the doll was gone, leaving only the discolored grass. "Where did the doll vanish to so quickly?" asked Claude. Though he was an expert in paranormal situations, this shocking event had left him puzzled.

During all the cases for which he investigated before, not even one of his them had a direct impact on his family.

Sophia, as a devoted mother, asked her children to report any reappearance of the doll and, if seen, everyone was forbidden to touch, or come into direct contact with it."

All the children, except Myriam replied, "Yes Mom. We will follow your instructions."

As for Myriam, she was possessed by the spirit that was haunting the doll. She replied, "Mom the beauty of the doll is something I had never saw before. I am just wondering why such beauty could put me in eminent danger."

Claude replied, "Well, my dear little one, I know you do not understand everything. I remember, when I was your age, I was just like you. I wanted to be challenged; I found pleasure in it. This doll is nothing to play with."

"That's true, Dad," replied Myriam, innocently. "Our family has seen so many different challenges, and we always come out on top."

Claude and Sophia were deeply affected by the tenacity of their younger daughter. Could it be the nail in the coffin for their family; was it in too early a stage to determine?

Finally, they all walked back to the mansion. Dinnertime was just around the corner, and the little army was starting to get hungry. Soon enough, the children forgot all about the mysterious doll, and they changed the subject on the beautiful time they had prior to the discovery.

The family was seated around their table, and they enjoyed the fresh meal that was served to them.

***

During that time back in the world of fiction and reality, disaster was taking place in the beautiful, well-hidden garden.

PETRONAS and the crazy lady were in a heated argument. At one point, PETRONAS remembered the fictional aspect of the crazy lady. Time was marching ahead and, soon, they would be separated by distance, but not by spirit.

PETRONAS solemnly announced to the crazy lady that a curse would be cast upon the beauty of natural appearance of the hidden garden.

"Just like you have asked me to cast a spell upon your doll, I am forced to do the same to this beautiful and peaceful place; it is to succumb to the spell of devastation."

The crazy lady jumped up exclaimed, "What are you talking about? How is this beautiful, relaxing garden linked to the spell cast upon my beloved doll?"

PETRONAS replied, "Lady, just as what you are impersonating, this garden is fiction. However, it is a fiction that will progressively become a reality."

In shock, the crazy lady replied, "You are telling me that, one day, someone will come to find this garden gate?"

"Yes," replied PETRONAS. "When this person comes to find this hidden gate, there will be a sad situation where your doll will be the cause of the devastation."

The crazy lady replied, "PETRONAS, remember, I paid you the hard price for the service you have rendered me, and I expect for you to respect our engagement, and rule."

"What are you talking about, lady? I am the one who has set the rules and demands. You are the one who came to me. begging and submissive. By the way, what engagement are you referring to? I am not the one who came to you. Let me remind you that you were the one who begged to receive my services.

"By far, I am a cruel, and demanding, spell caster and, once service of this caliber has been requested, and octroyed, from me, nothing comes in between. There is no more place for compassion or understanding. Once the deal is done, it becomes sealed. The price tag never diminishes, and the recipient's responsibilities never come to an end.

"With that said, it is time to take action and end this conversation. There's no use to trying to avoid the momentary destruction of this beautiful garden which, I say, must say perish."

The crazy lady was trembling in terror. She had nowhere to hide, nor had she one iota of a chance to find common ground finding between her and her chosen master.

After a moment of reflection, PETRONAS took the conversation in a new direction, so much that the crazy lady became suspiciously doubtful. "You know, dear lady," said PETRONAS "You are only one little peon that I use, every day, to protect my interest, and my investment.

"Yes, you will become my investment as you fully surrender to my will, and my guise. Sometimes, this will require an unwilling submission on your part. This beautiful garden will be restored to its previous beauty, just as your lovely doll will also be delivered from the spell, I was forced to cast upon it.

"These events will occur at the same time. I know, very well, that it may surprise you hearing me telling you these things because you know you are fictitious. However, the little girl who will fall in love with your doll will be a real person dealing with the consequence of your role as an involuntary slave to the unique situation.

"The time will come when I will be confronted. As I told you previously, I am sure you will remember that, while seated at the restaurant table, I mentioned how I will be forced, and physically challenged, by the father of the little girl.

"Let me tell you, it will be a harsh and cruel dual, and the father, with his perseverance and dedication for his family, will force me to let go.

"That day, I will, if I can, express myself this way, die and disappear forever, just like you, today, will set foot into your last residence. Your role, and presence, will no longer be needed because I, your master, would have been overthrown. But, until then, I must execute my evil wishes, and guise, ensuring that every little detail is fulfilled, and executed.

"Now, as I am about to destroy this garden. I am asking you to step out of the gate leading to it. Before your eyes, you will witness a pitiful work created by, and for, deception. Yes, I will cast the spell of dead upon every flower and tree and everything that moves in this lovely place."

Terrified, the crazy lady followed the instructions of PETRONAS and, as she was making her way out of the garden, she conserved the paradise in the corner in her mind.

The crazy lady was upset at having to be the first to witness such work of destruction. She knew, by experience, that PETRONAS was an expert in casting spells.

She stepped out of the garden and was standing by the gate to witness the work of destruction.

Before casting his spell, PETRONAS had a commotion between fiction and reality; he was affected by the unprecedented event that he was just about to perform.

After having taken one long look at the secret garden, PETRONAS glanced in the direction of the crazy lady and said, "Right after I have finished casting the spell, you will be on your way to your last home where, as I promised, you would die a holy life. But, before this event occurs, you will be vested by some gifts that will earn you honor, and respect, so much you will be considered a savior.

"From time to time, I shall visit you. At first, you may not recognize me, but it will not take a whole lot of time until you do. You will have to carry this secret with you and not divulge, to anyone, my real identity. If, by mischance you reveal my identity, you will be punished, right then and there."

The crazy lady asked PETRONAS how she would find her way to the convent; she thought that it would be a good question to embarrass PETRONAS. Empowered by her apparent victory, the crazy lady was impatiently waiting for PETRONAS's answer.

In fact, PETRONAS seemed, for the first time, to be caught off guard. For a moment, the crazy lady savoured the moment, as she was hopeful to have thrown in one attack that was insolvable to her adversary.

With a quick nod at the crazy lady, PETRONAS let her know that he was on top of the situation.

For a moment, there was some suspense following PETRONAS's action. That moment was to be crucial for the next stage of the haunting of the cottage because two factors would have to operate all at once.

***

Claude was now reading the chapter about the famous train which no one was able to move. Why it was stalled was a great mystery.

Claude's children, however, noticed that there was smoke coming out of the mufflers, and they were nervously running their way toward the family mansion.

"Dad, Dad, Dad!" they shouted. "Moms look at this! Oh, man, the train is leaving, driven by an invisible driver!"

Sophia ran out the front door entry, and Claude rushed out of his room. Both parents were standing nervously at the threshold of the mansion.

As for the children, they were stupefied, and almost horrified, by the phenomenon.

"Well," said Claude, "this means that we now have to call on the town authorities to investigate what is going on. Maybe this is the invisible thief who is responsible for all the supernatural occurrences in this cottage."

That was the first time that Claude had mentioned seeking help from the local authorities; he was that affected by the twist of events. Sure enough, a loud sound came out of the rusty horn of the locomotive to indicate that it was running, almost sounding like it was laughing at the confusion that it was creating.

Not much long after, the train took off. The officials of the town were entering the cottage, and Claude went over to greet them.

At first, the officers were speechless at seeing Claude come forward.

"Hello," said a nervous Claude. "And… yes, the train took off without any given warning. My children were out in the yard; they were the first ones to witness the event."

The lead officer replied, "We'll, let's ask them if they noticed anything different, like some intruders secretly entering the train which sat idle for so long and no one could ever make run."

"Sure," said Claude. "I am sure they will help with your investigation."

Claude, accompanied by the city official, entered the mansion where, a long time ago, the first investigation took place.

The children were just as shocked at having seen the train take off. They were practically trembling, like they wanted to leave, because they had no other information to give.

They were playing in the yard when, suddenly, Eric called for his siblings to notice the dark smoke coming out the muffler of the train.

The officers were taken off guard, and mysteries were empowering the evil curse cast upon the cottage. The whole town was suddenly on edge. Everyone ran for security, not knowing that the dearest consequence that they would have to pay.

During that time, PETRONAS solemnly replied to the crazy lady, "Just wait, here is your ticket for your entry to the convent." At the precise moment, the train was arriving near the gate of the garden.

"Hurry, we do not have much time now because the whole town, and all the officers, are on alert and are now investigating the mysterious disappearance of the famous train.

Seeing the train, the crazy lady almost fainted. She saw that the drivers of the train were the boys whom she had murdered. "Where will this boy drive me?" the crazy lady asked. "Will this boy finally drive me to insanity, although, I am already a non-existent crazy lady?"

PETRONAS ordered the crazy lady to step onto the train.

The boy had opened the entry.

The crazy lady was nervous, and irate. However, she submitted to the order of PETRONAS.

Once she had boarded the train, PETRONAS, for the last time, solemnly said, "Before this is all over, here is the last thing you will do for the rest of your miserable life."

Suddenly, PETRONAS lifted his hand and, like a sign of provocation, a ray a light appeared. PETRONAS, at the gate of the now cursed garden, invoked the dark spirit of dead to descend and enter the lovely haven. The beautiful garden became ravaged by the spirit of death; where once everything was radiant with life, everything was overshadowed by the work of dead.

At that precise moment, a sword and a crown appeared in the ray of light. The beautiful garden then became a work of destruction.

PETRONAS looked at the crown and the sword. "This is the sword of vengeance. This precious metal will be the rejuvenator, bringing justice to the garden, but you shall come with a price, a dire duel between love and hate."

The crazy lady now was speechless; troubled by the twisted final moment that she had with her master.

Waving his right hand as a sign of goodbye, PETRONAS said, "Farewell, crazy lady. Also, welcome. You will forever be destroyed after having lived a holy life in the convent. Your real identity will be revealed only after you pass away."

Then, the train continued to its destination.

As for PETRONAS, he disappeared into thin air, just like a ghost; he was now nowhere to be seen.

During the trip back to her last home, the crazy lady was now at the hands of the boys whom she had murdered boys; she was compliant. She knew that it was all over, the final moment of her fake existence.

Chapter 8
Claude's family victimized

Claude told the police about a strange crazy lady who had lived next to his home. "Maybe she is part of a scam. Sometimes, I feel like this woman is not even a real person. I just don't know how to put it into words."

The officer replied to Claude, "You are not the only one who came to us with this observation. All of the former owners packed up their belongings after having recovered whatever money they could within legal means."

"It is true, I have been warned that this place was the subject of maledictions," said Claude. "My career is to correct situations like this but, so far, I've never seen such a work of destruction. My promise to you, and the town, is I will unveil the culprit behind this mystery."

Just when Claude finished the last sentence, the realtor who sold the place was pulling into the driveway. He had been alerted by a close friend about the disturbance occurring, and he had noticed that the train was nowhere to be seen.

"Well, a pleasure to see you back here," Claude said, shaking the hand of the realtor.

"Looks you are having some strange events occurring," said the realtor.

"Yes," replied Claude. "These just happened not too long ago, like only a couple of hours."

"When the train disappeared, were you able to get it started, and moving?"

"No," replied Claude. "The train has a mind of its own. I was in my room, and my children were the ones who saw the monster running and getting ready to take off."

The realtor told Claude to use precaution because he remembered one of the former owners telling him about the day that the train would move by itself.

"Well," replied Claude. "Thank you for the information. I will watch over my family. We will prepare for any situation that may come up to give us hardship. By the way," said a proud Claude. "We were challenged before, and we found our way through the pile of misery intended for our family."

One of the officers asked Claude, "How many times have you dealt with supernatural circumstances like these?"

"To be honest with you, this is the first time I have seen such a wonder, and a puzzle. It is true that I have come across different situations where I could understand, or almost feel, the mysterious force behind the disastrous ordeal. But why the train took off by itself brings my curiosity to another level."

Another officer asked Claude if he ever had to deal with some bad curse, or tragedy, inflicted directly upon his young children.

Claude replied, "I can understand your concern about my children. Let me tell you, I have never come across any direct challenge where my own children found themselves directly involved."

Claude's last statement was proving to be false now. He knew that his younger daughter was affected by the beauty of the doll. He also knew that, if the doll was always blindfolded , his daughter was out of immediate danger.

Now, with the doll having made its appearance, Claude was more precautious, and alert. He had already read many chapters in the fascinating book that he borrowed from the town library.

He remembered the tension with the librarian, how strangely she had reacted when he said that he was researching the house. Claude thought that there must be more information that could be retrieved so he could make an honest assessment regarding the magnitude of the situation haunting the cottage.

The lead officer, after having examined the location where the train was sitting for so long, told Claude, "I trust your judgment, and I also know you will be able to solve this puzzle.

"I have done some research since you bought the cottage and, so far, no one better than you could react to this nonsense happening here. When you first expressed your desire to buy the cottage, we at the police department were in disbelief and had given you far less credit that you deserve and have earned.

"I remember thinking, *this will be just one other person to come and try to live here. Then, after the bad luck and on his way out, he will never set foot back into our community.*"

"Just like so many former owners, I personally judged you without knowing all the facts," said another officer.

After that admission, Claude was pleased to see that his efforts, and tenacity, had made a big impact upon the town, and its habitants. Claude was proud to have proven all the prejudices wrong.

After a moment, the lead officer told Claude that it was time for them to leave and resume their other duties, reaffirming to Claude that he had one hundred percent support from the police administration.

"Feel free to call us at any time you need our help. I can assure you that our prompt and diligent assistance will be given to you."

The officers drove away. It was a big deal for the police force because the train that had been dormant for so many years had finally moved again.

The press had released a warning to the entire town to be on the lookout for the train and, if the train was located, to notify the town officials immediately.

During that time, Claude was mortified by the tenure of the last unpredicted event, and he was trying to find a solution.

Sophia was exhorting her children not to enter the train, although she understood that it would be tempting for them to do so. Another problem was on the horizon for Claude's family; it was a situation where the whole heart would be submitted to cruel, and unfair, treatment.

They would have no other choice but to suffer dire consequences, and headaches, until Claude unveiled the secrets that would prompt their deliverance and forever end the evil spell cast onto the cottage.

Claude's mind was on the doll that appeared from nowhere just before the whole ordeal had started. Maybe this doll was the culprit, the mastermind behind the mystery causing panic among his family.

That night, the children refused to go play outside, afraid of anything moving, suspicious of every little noise that they may have heard. It was the beginning of a chaotic situation. The toll of stress was dominant, replacing the peaceful atmosphere.

The children even found it hard to go places on their own property during the perfect sunny days.

Myriam, however, was an adventurous character. She did not appreciate the reluctance of her other siblings to go explore the rest of their property. Like a brave little girl, she said, "If no one wants to come with me outside, I will be going by myself."

Sophia did not like the idea of Myriam's tenacity of pursuing her taste for adventure. "I have only one wish, and it is that my younger daughter was born without this burning taste for adventure, especially while we are under such pressure."

Finally, after having raising hell, Sophia let Myriam step outside under strict rules, leaving her other older siblings in charge.

Myriam was on her way to the barn; she was enjoying her time spent alone while her older brother, who stood on the balcony to supervise her activity.

Claude was back in his room, continuing his reading; it was hard for him to focus his attention only on the chapter that he was reading.

Sure enough, not long after Myriam received the okay to step out after having agreed to follow the rules that her mother had given her, she perceived the doll. No one other than her saw it because the doll faced the behind wall of the family home.

The wise little Myriam stopped for a minute. She knew that, if she said something about the presence of the doll, she would not be allowed out again for the rest of the day. So, Myriam decided to act like nothing had happened. The atmosphere was heavy. Sophia was nervous that she had finally allowed her younger daughter to step out.

To Myriam's surprise, the doll took off and left behind her a trail leading to the island.

She decided to follow the path that the doll had left for her. Her little heart was unevenly beating, yet her desire for adventure was predominant.

Myriam arrived at the island. Feeling relaxed, she let her guard down and started to explore what the island had to offer.

There was an old shack standing on the middle of the island. It was the first time that Myriam had set foot on the island all by herself, and a surprise was awaiting her.

The infamous doll was in the middle; it sat on the chair of the table in the main room. There was also an antique bedframe with an old mattress.

"There you are, "Myriam said. "Oh, you are such a beauty. Why do you have your eyes blinded?"

After having waiting for a few minutes, the enthusiastic child's curiosity made it so that she was dying to see what color the doll's eyes were.

Myriam was too young to realize the danger that she was facing. Overcome by the beauty of the doll, she was dying to see the color of its eyes. She approached the doll put her hand on it. She then waited for a few seconds to realize that nothing bad had happened. Myriam stepped back a little to consider the doll one more time and, at that precise moment, she was entrapped by PETRONAS's spell.

Delicately, she took the doll in her hand and untied the knot behind its eyes.

Shortly after, the piece of cloth which had covered the doll's eyes fell onto the floor. Myriam turned it around and, for the first time, she saw the doll's eyes, and they were blue.

Immediately following her eye contact with the blue, glass eyes of the doll, Myriam felt ill. She went to lie down on the old bed, falling into a deep sleep. She became the victim of the crazy lady who Myriam with her taste for adventure was the chosen one to suffer a dire price.

***

During that time, Sophia became extremely worried about where her younger daughter was. She asked Julian to walk around the house to see what his sister was doing.

"Sure, Mom, I will do that" he replied.

Julian started by calling Myriam several times, but with no answer. Julian then became nervous; it was not like Myriam to not respond when called.

Julian walked into the nearby building, only to discover that his little sister was nowhere to be found. As Julian was crossing to go over to the powerhouse, he noticed a bright light coming from the island. He could not believe what he was witnessing.

Julian ran back to the mansion.

Sophia became nervous because she knew that, if Julian was so out of breath, then it was for a serious reason. The sudden disappearance of the train was still fresh in her memory and, every time she walked out, it was as if the train wanted to remind her that it was gone. "What is happening? Did you see Myriam? Is she in trouble?"

Julian had a hard time keeping his emotions to himself. "Mom, I don't know where Myriam is. I have looked everywhere I could and still no trace of her. As I was coming around to the powerhouse, I saw a bright light shining over from the island."

Claude heard this from the other room. He jumped out of his chair ran like the speed of the light to the kitchen, were Sophia, Julian, and two of his other kids were.

Right away, he noticed that the atmosphere was tense. Claude nervously asked if Myriam was all right, furious at his wife for having let her go out all by herself.

Sophia, on the defensive, acknowledged her lack of judgment. "I didn't want Myriam to go by herself, but she became so unbearable I sent her out, supervised by her brother."

Claude replied, "I am very afraid about your lack of judgment. I am afraid that we are just about to experiment a catastrophic event, and this kind will be a first. Let us go out and see what our younger daughter is doing. Hopefully, she just playing hide and seek. We know, all too well, about her love for challenging situations." Claude stepped out of the mansion and began looking around the front yard.

After having called Myriam a couple of times with no answer, Sophia froze. At that moment, she observed the bright light coming from the island adjoining the property. Eric looked at the right side of the mansion and exclaimed, "Oh, come on, Dad! Come and see this bright light, maybe...."

Claude did not let Eric finish his last sentence rush. "Oh, for goodness sake, this is more serious than I thought it would be," Claude said, nervously.

Not sure what to expect, the worried father ordered everyone to get inside the mansion as he, himself, stepped in.

Sophia was shaking like a leaf.

Eric and Jessica ran to her side. "Mom," they asked, "are we in danger? We have been through many situations before, but nothing like this one."

During that time, Claude walked into his room closed the book, and prepared to walk over to the island to investigate the bright light. He then asked Julian if he wanted to come with him.

Julian replied, "Yes, Dad. I am ready to go with you. Anything I can do to help my little sister; I will be happy to do so."

Sophia did not like the idea of her husband bringing her son. "Are you out of your mind? We already have one of our children possibly missing. Are you seriously secure taking our son with you?"

After a moment of hesitation, Claude replied, "I understand this is a big gamble; I am not sure if this is the right thing to do. However, I would not deprive our older son the opportunity to come to the rescue of his little sister.

"Maybe Myriam has staged a false disappearance. And, if this is the case, we have nothing to lose, but everything to gain, from Julian's presence. I am sure Myriam's love for her older brother will prevail."

"Dad," replied Julian. "I was on the balcony all along while she was walking around the front yard and entered the barn. I do not recall seeing her coming out of the barn. Besides, Mom told me to keep an eye opened since she let her go outside."

"Let us follow the footprints. Maybe she is hidden somewhere, or she fell and hurt herself."

With caution, Claude, followed by Julian, followed the fresh footprints on the ground. "Looks to me Myriam was not abducted," said Claude. "Maybe she is playing hide and seek."

As they were approaching the island, Julian called for his sister. "This is strange," said Julian. "I've never known my little sister not to come when called."

Finally, Claude and Julian arrived at the island with no indication as to where Myriam could be; the bright light that they observed from the mansion had diminished a little. The trail was as fresh, as if it was made just a couple of seconds ago.

They arrived at the end of the trail and entered the shack. Claude walked into the little house, toward the straw bed mattress where Myriam was lying. He called her name, but she did not respond. Upon closer inspection, Claude saw that she had been turned to wax.

"My goodness," said Claude. "Myriam, what happened to you?"

Father and son looked around for any clues as to why Myriam was lying on the bed, like a wax statue. Her face was beautiful, and her hair fresh.

Julian said, "Dad, Myriam is not dead. If she was, then she wouldn't be looking so beautiful."

Claude nervously replied, "Son, I forbid you to touch her. That might only add to the curse."

After a moment of scrutiny, Claude and Julian were taken by surprise when they heard a noise coming from the direction of the desk sitting in the middle of the shack.

Claude rushed over to see what could have been the cause of the noise. To his surprise, he noticed the fresh imprint of the doll, like she was sitting on the chair.

"Be careful, Julian," said Claude. "It appears we are not alone."

After having removed the chair from its original position, father and son could clearly envision the scenario; it was not a good sign.

Having secured the bed were Myriam was "sleeping," Claude walked out of the shack. Claude and Julian then began walking side by side around the house but could not find anything out of the ordinary.

Claude lifted up his head to cry out, "Whoever you are, spirit, reveal yourself to me. If you want to fight, do not hide from me, like a coward. You started this; now it is time for you to put all the cards onto the table."

Just as Claude finished his plea, Julian noticed the famous doll. "Look at this, Dad. The spirit tormenting us heard you."

Chapter 9
Trailing the Doll

After closing the door of the shack, Claude and Julian started their journey of chasing the suspected doll that had transferred the curse onto Myriam.

After Claude ran toward the moving doll, he noticed that its eyes had been uncovered.

"Oh, no!" exclaimed a furious Claude. "I just knew my daughter would not be able to resist the temptation."

Looking at the doll, Claude said, "And, you, my dear. Wait till I get hold of you! I am sure, by now, the spirit haunting you knows I possess some knowledge about your hidden secret. Yes, I have found the key and, now, I am sure you will make me pay a dire price for the recovery of my daughter."

Julian stayed behind his father at Claude's request; the boy wanted so much to grab the doll and smash it to pieces. Julian was sure the doll was part of some hidden, dark secret to curse the family.

Claude knew the intentions of his son and told not to approach, or touch, the doll. "Son, I promise you I will render justice, and we will be victorious."

***

Claude and Julian arrived at the family mansion. Sophia was pleased to see her older boy entering the house. With a trembling voice, Claude announced to his wife that they had found Myriam.

Sophia reached the door of the mansion saying, "Where?"

Claude spoke to Sophia to let her know that Myriam was in deep distress. However, he wasn't sure what they could do to come to her rescue." Just before leaving the family home, Claude asked Julian to keep an eye on his brother and sister. He also said to make sure that the doors were all locked.

"Yes, Dad," replied Julian. "You can count on me. I will be alert so that nothing bad happens to any of us. I hope you won't be there for too long."

"No, Son. I will be right back to tell you the next steps to be taken. In the meantime, tell the others what took place to prepare them. I know they will want to see their younger sister but, for now, it is too soon.

"We have to come up with a plan of action, then we will all visit Myriam. Maybe then this drama will be over."

Just before leaving the mansion, Claude attached a flagpole to the balcony and asked Julian to raise the flag to alert them if anything was going wrong.

Sophia and Claude were on their way to the island.

Rapidly, they arrived, and Claude explained to his wife about the tragedy that had happened before he entered the shack.

As soon Claude had the door opened, Sophia rushed over to the old bed, where Myriam seemed to be sleeping, but not dead.

"Oh, my!" said the loving mother. "What happened to you, my dear little Myriam? Why did you come here by yourself? Didn't I tell you do not leave the surroundings of the mansion?"

Sophia now knew the doll had something to do with the catastrophic event. "Claude, what will be the next move now that the doll's eyes are exposed?"

"I am not sure, my dear. Rest assured, I will do everything in my power to find this doll and take care of business before another member of our family falls victim to this evil. I must return to the mansion before the other kids panic. In the meantime, you are free to stay here with Myriam."

"Yes," replied Sophia. "I will stay here with my daughter. Maybe she will wake up and see her mother at her side."

Claude replied, "That would be the ideal situation. In the meantime, I will take the rest of the children with me to the village and alert the police, and the doctor, so he can visit our daughter."

Claude begged his wife to not touch their daughter before a medical report has been made. He did not want to lose her to the affliction imposed upon him and his beloved family.

After having a look at her daughter, Sophia said, "Yes, Claude, I will not."

After hugging his wife, Claude began his journey back to the mansion; he was pleased to see that Julian had not raised the flag as a sign for distress.

On his way to the family mansion, Claude's mind was already planning the next step to recover Myriam.

He arrived at the mansion and found the children quietly seated around the family table.

After a few minutes with his family, Claude told them that he was going to town. He then asked them to get ready. With a lot on everyone's mind, and the heavy atmosphere, Claude and his children were anxious while on their way to the police station.

***

The town was primitive compared to most others; horse carriages and steam locomotives were still used to commune. Government agencies, like the police and a few of the town dignities, had the luxury of driving a car, whereas most of the island citizens did not. Since Claude had his own car, he was considered a dignitary by the whole town.

He arrived at the police station. After having parked his vehicle, Claude and his children entered the building to talk to an officer.

The officer at the front desk asked Claude what he could do to help him, not knowing the fragility of the reason why the family was at the police station.

"I need to talk to an investigator," replied Claude. "I have a major event to report, and I am sure it is not the first time that someone has reported about the cottage I bought not terribly to long ago."

After a moment, an officer introduced himself as John after a warm handshake. "How can I help you?" he asked.

For the first time, Claude was overwhelmed with emotion. He just could not hold onto his pride, and tears rolled down on his face. "Officer, my words are refusing to come out so much, as I am deeply affected."

After great effort, he told the officer that his daughter was found after he vigilantly searched her whereabouts under a spell cast on their cottage.

A compassionate officer replied, "You know, Claude, I admire your dedication, and love, for your family; doing such a good work in such dangerous career."

Claude said, "Officer, my younger daughter, Myriam, is not dead. She is lying beautifully in an old bed in an old shack. She disobeyed the order she received from us, and she took off the cloth from the doll's eyes." At that moment, Claude was glued to his chair, frozen, he felt the deepest of the vast ocean of despair that engulfed him.

With compassion, John replied, "Claude, we will do everything in our power, utilizing the latest technology we have at our disposition. I am sure, at the end of the journey, Myriam will be safe and sound.

"I have to tell you, just before you came here, we received a couple of notices that the doll has been in different places. The report stated that the eyes of the haunted doll were exposed to the view of everyone."

Claude replied nervously, "And, now, I suppose I will be blamed for every bad situation occurring in the town? Just because my younger daughter was not able to refrain from giving into her taste for adventure?"

John replied, "I know, right now, that you are in deep despair and wondering if our law enforcement agents are your bridge to justice. Let me reassure you, no one will ever know how the doll's eyes were seen by everyone who may have come into direct contact with it. Frankly, it would be hard to prove in court of law because anyone can be a child of curiosity in this unknown future."

Claude's mind was preoccupied by the fate of his daughter. Taking a deep breath, he replied to the officer. "During my entire career of the supernatural situations I investigated, never I, or my immediate family, became the target.

"The situation plaguing our cottage is, by far, more vicious, and controlling, than anything I came across, even in places where ghosts could be felt, or heard."

"Now you understand why, when you inquired about the beautiful cottage, that we warned you," replied John.

"Yes," replied Claude. "And I also remember all the warnings you gave to my family, but I guess this was bound to happen sometime.

"My wife and I will ensure that our Myriam, if she comes out of her self-imposed spell, will know we were there, twenty-four hours, a day looking out for her and her safety.

"I already have convened with my wife and have set up a continuing presence on the island. We have family members who are ready to step up and provide their assistance, and expertise, while we work together to overthrow the spell cast upon my daughter."

"That, in itself, is the wisest plan you and your wife could have come up with, finding support among your family first," replied John.

Claude asked the officer if there were any previous circumstances like theirs.

"Yes," John replied. "Our records showed us, and other authorities of the town, that there were a couple similar situations."

Claude asked the officer if those records were accessible. Maybe there were some clues in the others' files.

"Yes," replied John. "That can be arranged. I will make sure to make these records availed to you but, in the meantime, we must act.

"Here is my plan of action. We will ensure the privacy of your family. We will also work on this case as if one of our own children was the victim of such a cowardly, criminal act. We will also ensure that it does not occur against pledging to work one on one with you and your family.

It was moment of intense, wild thoughts, and wonder, reaching into the mind of a father and of the authority of the town.

"Well," said Claude. "I appreciate all the help, and every offer of help, you are giving me and my family. I will be working, together, with your department. I guess I have to go and ask the doctor to come visit my daughter and see what he could do to speed up the process of healing."

"That sounds like a good start," said the officer. "In the meantime, I will alert everyone on my taskforce to be on the lookout for this doll."

The men shook hands, then both returned to their busy schedule. Claude's children were especially happy to be on their way home so they could see their little sister.

Driving by the restaurant, Claude's children asked their father if they could stop and eat, as they were hungry.

Claude replied, "Yes, we will stop at the restaurant to get some food."

Soon after, the more somber family car was driving into a parking space at the restaurant.

Just before stepping out of the car, Claude asked his children to make it a quick and reminded them that their mother was likely worried. Claude's tone of voice indicated to his children that he was visibly shaken.

The restaurant owner came to greet Claude and his family. The news of the bizarre events, mixed with rumors, were already circulating in the town, especially with the train apparently being operated by a ghost.

Claude was listening to every word that the restaurant owner said. It was a fact that, since the errant train was driven by unknown forces, Claude's who were neighbors of the crazy lady, had not seen her around. They were happy because of this; no one in Claude's family really liked living next to her.

While Claude and his children were eating, the restaurant owner sat by their table and continued to express his opinion, as well as the latest discoveries made by the town official.

"You know, Claude, the town authorities are cautioning everyone about a possible disturbance in the town created by the influence of the doll. They also warn every parent to keep their eyes open, and it was suggested, and considered, a mandatory curfew be put in place for a short of period."

They owner of the restaurant was animated about the idea of a curfew imposed upon every family of the town.

Claude took a deep breath after looking at his children and replied, "Thank you for giving me the opportunity to know how the whole town reacted to the latest event. I would prefer you talk to me personally. As you can see, my children have a hard time with all the information you shared with us. They don't deserve to be reminded of this stressful situation."

The restaurant owner replied, "Fair enough with me. I will chat with you later I have so much more information to give you, and I am also curious to know your take on this whole situation."

After he finished drinking his coffee, the restaurant owner resumed his regular duties.

Claude and the children were in hurry to finish eating so they could return to their family home.

Claude's last stop was to the family doctor, to urge him to make a house call for his younger daughter.

The doctor said that he was free, so he followed Claude back to the cottage.

The family arrived back at their mansion, with the doctor in tow. It was not the first time that he was asked to render a visit to this house. On previous occasions, the doctor was called into the mansion for several cases, where members of the family occupying the mansion became inexplicably sick.

It was the first time that the doctor entered the mansion to notice that no one was victim to a suspicious health situation; he was not ready to envision anything worse.

After a brief exchange between Claude and the doctor, the children were ready to walk with their father and the doctor to the island.

On their way to their destination, some verbal exchanges of prudence and vigilance were the main topic. Although the children were young, they understood the gravity of the situation plaguing their sister and, quite possibly, their own lives.

The doctor now was just about to witness pure evil at work.

***

They traveled one mile to get to the island, where a concerned Sophia sat next to the primitive bed made of straw.

Sophia heard some noises coming from outside of the shack. She took the broom and lay it by herself, ready to use it as a weapon against any intruders who might try to come inside.

Sophia realized that it was her husband, accompanied by the rest of her family, setting foot onto the island; she also noticed the doctor's presence.

"Good," said Sophia "maybe the doctor will be able to diagnose, and prescribe, a cure for the bizarre sickness my daughter was cursed with."

Myriam was there, lying on the straw bed, never departing from her beauty. It was almost as if the doll's beauty was imprinted onto her body.

After she hugged her husband and shook hands with the family doctor, Claude asked Sophia if there were any new developments that she may have observed during his absence.

"No," replied Sophia. "Did the children have something to eat?"

"Yes," replied Claude. "I brought them to the town restaurant, where I learned that rumors of our misfortune were already circulating."

"Oh, my," replied Sophia. "And you, doctor, can you come up with some medical explanation as to what happened to my daughter? I know there was a curse cast upon her."

The doctor walked toward the bed, where Myriam was lying peacefully, and beautifully. He took her right hand, and, to his surprise, it had some vital signs. "Well, Myriam is still alive, but her pulse is very weak. It looks to me like she has been induced into a deep coma, and she has lost all sense of time."

After a couple more tests, the doctor confirmed that their daughter was, in fact, under a spell. The only remedy availed to this kind of sickness was patience, and faith.

"At this point," said the doctor putting back his stereoscope around his neck, "all I can tell you is don't let your daughter be without supervision. Maybe the culprit will be curious enough to come back to witness his cruelty.

"Almost all criminals, at one point or another, come back to the place where they commit their crime, and it gives them satisfaction to see that their projected plan has succeeded."

"Yes," replied Claude. "For me, it's only common sense. In the meantime, I am simply curious to know if there is anything specific science has to offer for cases like this."

The doctor replied, "I am afraid there is nothing that could be of any help from science. It is the other way around; science could only benefit from this experience.

"This is the first time I was ever a witness to such a tragedy. Nevertheless, I am sure whoever, or whatever, caused this to happen eventually will be apprehended by law enforcement."

"Thank you for coming here for the sake of our daughter, doctor," Claude said. "You know, the whole town is now aware of the situation going on here.

With all the traffic coming in and out of my cottage, this has surely got the attention of everyone.

"I feel like my privacy, and the privacy of my family, has been breached by rubberneckers, the media, and just plenty of curious villagers. I know this mansion has given itself a name over the years, so that no one dared to challenge. If they did, they walked away from it after dire defeat."

"Well, I hope I will be able to help you end this traumatic situation. I know that this will not be an easy task to curb the curse that this cottage is plagued with but, with your courage and love, you will prevail against this apparent unachievable project" said the doctor.

After a brief pause, Claude let his feelings resurface. With his wife at his side, tears were the only expression that replaced words. Claude, Sophia, and their children were in for the long hall of wonders, love, faith, and commitment.

Sophia gathered up her courage and told her husband that she would do everything within her power to ease their children's pain and distress.

The doctor excused himself as he shook Claude's hand. "I must go for now. Rest assured; I will be supporting you all the way through victory. I have faith, and confidence, in you."

Shortly after, the doctor was on his way back to his office, and Claude was left alone on the island, facing the rude reality that his daughter was now cursed.

CHAPTER 10
PETRONAS AT WAR

While the crazy lady arrived at her last destiny, the spirit of the little boy who was murdered because of her evil act had an interesting conversation with his murderer.

"You know, lady, I know you are just a fictious being, using a physical appearance to engulf in your evil this beautiful cottage where you murdered me.

"This beautiful, majestic property was never at fault, yet everyone blamed *it* when *you* walked away without leaving a trace. Now, there is just one individual whose courage, and determination, will destroy you forever.

"Your evil has reached its end. Now, it is time for you to be expelled from this paradise so we, your victims, can make peace and go on with our afterlives.

"I am the voice of the father you murdered who, unfortunately, has never been found. Yes, this noble father whom you pushed over the dam he owned was never retrieved from the deepest fathoms of the water. He floated his way out of his town to be forever separated from his family. This family left the cursed cottage soon after the mysterious disappearance.

"After years of internal pain and suffering, and the children got a little older, they were able to finally make peace with their cruel situation.

"One fine afternoon, they decided to visit their once family home, in search for clues as to where their father had vanished. They left the mansion, empty-handed, and broken-hearted, not able to put to rest this mystery haunting their family.

"It is true, the scenario of their father accidently falling down the dam was a possibility that no one envisaged seriously. That was because they knew their father was very agile; he was a good swimmer and would have not drowned, unless being set up by someone."

The crazy lady sat, transfixed, as she remembered some of her monstrous crimes. And, now, she was about to be revealed to the whole town. It became clear to the fictional crazy lady that she would finally lose her grip on the beautiful cottage.

The resident of the cottage would not hesitate, for one second, to demolish her residency where, for years, she was able to hide and deceive so many. Her deception was that she would be forever exposed as a fraud that finished her day into a convent that never existed.

The spirit of the little boy also talked about the other little boy who had innocently glued rocks to the bottom of her watering can and was also killed by her devilish vengeance. He stated that he was with him but remained invisible.

The train seemed to travel its way through time, in which the crazy lady was projected like a movie at the theater.

Taken off guard, the crazy lady went completely insane; she could not take the pressure of her past, fictional life. She knew that it was not making any sense. The crazy lady also knew that, because she was a fictional character with a physical, identical human body, she was also free from the barrier of a physical appearance.

The little boy took pleasure in reminding the treacherous, fake woman of the enormities, and calamities, that her supposed craziness had imposed for years upon an entire town.

***

During this time, Claude was preoccupied with the many challenges that the curse had presented to his whole family. Sophia was seen, every day, walking her way to the island, vigilantly overseeing her younger daughter's safety.

The whole town was now aware of the situation because of all the stories and rumors. Everyone was on high alert, and concern. The citizens vowed to help Claude and his family, in any way they could, during their time of need.

Horses from volunteer farmers were seen patrolling the rustic streets, loaded with wagons full of residents looking out to apprehend the culprit behind the sad occurrence.

The police department were also patrolling the street, going from house to house, questioning the citizens of the town if they knew anything about the crazy lady.

A couple of residents, like the store owner where the crazy lady purchased her dress, and the restaurant owner, had a lot of interesting stories to relay about the strange woman.

What about the mysterious disappearance of the librarian? She also went missing without leaving any trace; this was right around the same time the so-called fiction crazy woman disappeared.

There was also the famous train which, suddenly after years being out of service for unknown reasons, on that same day ran the rails to never came back.

The family doctor visited every day and documented the evolution of the bizarre situation. Not knowing how long the affliction would last, he, and his staff, were prepared for a long, and unpredictable, amount of work.

With the curse cast upon Myriam, the investigation had accelerated to the point where the family became the subject of good wishes, and sympathy.

The residents of the town rushed to the crazy lady's house and, after having inspected every inch of it, they received the green light to demolish the building. The house was creepy, like the kind one would see in a horror movie.

The authorities were hoping that, by demolishing the haunted house, it would accelerate the investigation, and the crazy lady who resided there would show up at any time. Claude was happy to see the house that he disliked so much being demolished, and forever erased from the village.

The night of the demolition went well. Nothing out of the ordinary was reported, except a deep feeling that the demolition of the house was the beginning of even more trouble. It was to be expected, as everyone considered the house odd and haunted.

The morning following the demolition, Claude suddenly felt sick, like he had the flu; his fever was running high. He told Sophia he suspected that it was because of the stress he had during the last couple of days.

After having finished preparing the breakfast, and the children cleaned the dishes, Sophia walked in the room where Claude was resting.

"Well, dear," she said. "I hope you feel better soon. Do you think this sickness you are experimenting now is part of the curse cast upon Myriam?"

Claude had thought about the possibility and, for the sake of his family, he chose to be brave and replied, "My dear Sophia, I know we are under enormous stress, and our family has more than its fair share to deal with.

"However, I will get better. By remaining brave and calm, with a positive attitude, we are countering the evil that terrorizes our family. We have faced many other situations where we came in direct contact with supernatural forces. This situation, by far, is not exempt of calamities."

The children gathered around their parents, ready to take upon the challenge indirectly imposed on them.

After they hugged their father, they were on their way, as usual, to the island with their mother. Their little sister's misfortune was the only thing that the children were able to think about, and it also haunted their dreams at night.

***

The family entered the shack one more time. Myriam was still lying there.

Sophia took a washcloth to wipe off any dust that may have landed on her daughter's face.

***

During that time, Claude read more of the mysterious book which he had borrowed from the town library. Once again, he was captivated by the concrete information that the ex-owner had taken the time to write down about their misfortune, and how it happened.

As he was reading the next chapter, Claude stumbled upon a claim that a secret entry was hidden in a fabulous garden. He was captivated by the description, which made him pause for a moment for reflection.

"This garden must be not to terribly far out," Claude said. "What amazes me the most is that we have yet discovered the secret entry, even though we have lived here for a good while now."

Like lightning, a brief thought crossed the mind of Claude. *We will, let see, maybe this is the missing piece of the puzzle.*

Claude had just finished reading the chapter in its entirety when a car pulled up into the driveway. "That must be the chief of police, or one of his investigators."

Claude took a moment to glance at the next chapter, which was called "The Culprit." He was happy because, now, he would find out where the culprit was hidden, and he intended to begin looking for him.

Claude put down the book and walked his way to greet the officer who was now standing in the doorway of the house. He proceeded to tell the officer that he was not feeling good enough for any outdoor activities that day.

The two men sat down around a table in the living room and discussed their recent findings in search for clues to the mystery of the doll haunting the town.

The officer pointed out to Claude he noticed that since the "crazy lady" was nowhere to be seen, the librarian was also missing in action. The officer added, "Who in the world would be mentally fit to see their house demolished and not inquire about the motive of such of an action? Maybe those two individuals are in cahoots with each other."

"Yes," replied Claude. "There are many questions and, yet, very few answers. I believe we are onto the right path. Patience it the ultimate tool we currently have in our reach to resolve this mystery, once and for all."

Just as Claude finished his statement, a loud horn sounded. "Wait," said Claude. "Did you hear the sound of a train whistle just now?"

"Yes, I sure did," replied the officer. "I suppose I have to get going now and investigate this new development." The officer said his goodbyes, left the mansion, and drove off to investigate the sudden sound of the train approaching town.

Upon the departure of the officer, Claude returned to his room, where he took a couple of hours to rest; he was feeling better already.

After taking some medication for his flu symptoms, he sat at his desk and continued reading the chapter which had captured his attention.

"The Culprit," said Claude. "Let us discover who the culprit of all this misery is." As he devoured every word and phrase in the chapter, Claude resumed putting the final pieces of the puzzle together.

***

It became a routine for Sophia and Claude to eat a modest dinner at the same table where Myriam uncovered the eyes of the haunted doll. A candle sat on a shelf near Myriam's pillow. The romantic scene seemed to enhance the girl's beauty, who looked as fresh as she does when come out of the shower.

The family doctor was faithful to his commitment, finding time, every day, to visit Myriam and talk with Sophia and Claude. He wrote his observations in his record book. Nothing out of the ordinary happened to Myriam after her transformation due to the spell cast upon her. For the doctor and Sophia, this was a good sign, as there was hope that she would be delivered soon.

***

Back at the mansion, Claude was absorbed with his reading so much that he was inhaling the chapter's contents. Every word that he read became like a part of his own life. That was when Claude discovered where the secret entry in the hidden garden was to be found. The way that the chapter was worded made it sound ambiguous, but Claude felt like he was so close to figuring it out.

Toward the end of the chapter, Claude was instructed that the person reading this chapter, while affected by a mysterious illness, should be the only one present at the hidden gate. *That sounds like a challenge for me,* Claude thought. Maybe this garden could be the residence of the culprit. *Better yet, it may show me the reason why this cottage was inhabitable.*

After pausing for a brief reflection, Claude remembered the sound of the haunted train which was trying to make its way back into town. He was connecting the dots together, just as the book was instructing him to, and it was like each new word had resonated in his mind as a solid clue.

***

The day was going by, and it was time for Sophia and the children to return to their home after being relieved by a close relative who volunteered to guard Myriam for the night. After having said goodbye to her youngest child, she and the children began to make their way back home.

Claude was happy to see his wife and children come home after having spent the entire day at the bedside of Myriam.

Sophia did not even have to prepare supper because some of the residents had sent a warm meal to help Claude and his family. Myriam's misfortune had invoked the sympathy of everyone in town.

That night was to be a turning point for Claude because he had almost solved the mysteries and the cause of their daughter's curse. Claude knew that he had to fight for his younger daughter without any help from the rest of his family.

During that time, the police continued their investigation with extraordinarily little new clues, and details, reported, except for reports from the town's inhabitant who complained about the noise of a train whistle, though no one had actually seen the train.

The days of Claude's family having peace and quiet were numbered, although everyone in town were respecting their privacy.

After supper was served, the children played in the front yard of the mansion; they found themselves in a world of wonders.

After her day of taking care of her younger daughter, Sophia sat by Claude's side. The conversation fell on to the day, and how the children were holding together.

Claude was proud of his family. "I wonder what I would do if I were in their little shoes. To me, they all deserve a medal of honor for their heroism."

Sophia replied, "I, myself, wonder how they take such of a load of deception day in and day out without complaining. Obviously, they are terribly affected to see their younger sister hit with such a sinister evil, yet their love for her prevails."

Claude took the occasion to tell his wife that he had made some remarkably interesting discoveries while he was not feeling good; he had spent half of his day reading the little book.

"From the chapter I just finished reading, it talks about a secret entry into a garden. However, it says, clearly, that the garden is the residence of an evil spirit. It does not come out and say that it is an evil spirit, but my conclusion is that may be this is the place where the spirit of deception hides."

"Oh, my!' replied Sophia. "And I suppose you are about to tackle this brutal force and obey the order from our author of misfortune. By the way, are you sure this is really the right interpretation of your reading?

"I suggest that someone other than you go over the entire text. This would ensure the integrity of your findings because I am wondering Myriam's situation is not playing a key role into your interpretation of your reading."

To that, Claude replied, "My dear Sophia, I understand your concern. Rest assured; I will not jump into conclusions without having a path toward victory."

The children had gone to bed for the night. Claude and Sophia walked toward their room after hugging them and telling them goodnight. Not too long after, the entire house was quiet. Everyone enjoyed the peacefulness of the night.

***

The morning arrived too soon, and the joyous family, once again, were up and running, getting a start on their duties. That morning, Sophia asked her husband if he intended to start his search for the mysterious entryway hidden somewhere near their cottage.

"Yes, my dear. I am resolute to find this gate. I am sure, over the years, this secret entry has been rendered invisible."

"Do me a favor," said the loving wife, "take at least one of your closest friends when you go on your way to find this interesting doorway to the secret garden."

"Yes," replied Claude. "I think this would be the right thing to do."

A visibly worried Sophia replied, "Please, be careful, Claude. Our children need their father to provide them with food, love, and comfort, as you have always done." After having hugged her husband, Sophia and the children were, once again, on their way to the island.

During that time, Claude was preparing to confront the spirit haunting his cottage.

***

After having reviewed the details revealed to him in the book, Claude felt that it was time for him to move into action but, before he engaged in a physical battle with the unknown, he paid a short visit one of his trusted friends.

It was Peter, who Claude had met shortly after the family moved into the mansion. During the time that Claude's family had lived on the island, the two of them had developed a strong relationship.

"Hello, Peter, I want to be short and sweet. I thought to let someone know today that I aim to confront the source of misery that this lovely cottage has been ravaged with."

Peter replied, "Oh, can I come with you? This is a serious, and delicate, mission you are undertaking."

Claude replied, "No, Peter, this is something I have to do all alone, according to the instructions presented to me in the book. I decoded the secret language of the book I found in the town library."

"Well, at least would you give me the location, in case something goes wrong? At least, I will know where to begin looking for you, and the location the event is taking place."

"Yes," replied Claude. "However, keep in mind that this is my estimate; I am solidly one hundred percent sure I am at the right location."

"Well," said an ecstatic Peter, "wherever you go, and whatever you do, be really careful. I do not want to lose your friendship for anything in the world."

Claude replied, "Yes, I will be incredibly careful. Here is the map of my calculations and the whereabouts where I will be during a short period of time." Claude gave Peter a description of the secret entryway into the hidden garden.

"Yes!" exclaimed Peter. "I forgot about this little detail; I was aware of this mysterious entryway into to a garden that was cursed long time ago. Be very careful, I am sure you are onto something big; maybe this will be the end of the tragedy that this lovely place is plagued with.

"I will be the first one to offer to buy the cottage from you after you have succeeded putting to rest this devilish curse."

After the brief exchange, Claude walked off to reach his destination. Now more than ever, he was convinced that he was on the right track.

Claude arrived at the entrance of an area overgrown with plants. He took a couple of steps into the forest.

Suddenly, something strange got his attention. There was a trail, and it resembled the one that he and Julian saw the first day when they were looking for Myriam; that led them to discover Myriam's location on the island.

Claude's heartrate increased after he took a close look at the fresh trail on the ground. He followed the fresh trail to wherever it would lead him, and it stretched farther than he could see in front of him.

After a good twenty minutes of walking in the woods, the trail suddenly vanished. For one quick minute, Claude was left puzzled in wonder, making him guess what to do next. "Well, let us look around. Maybe it is trying to tell me that the gate of this secret place is nearby."

After having closely surveyed his surroundings, Claude discovered a thinner spot that could quite possibly be a doorway.

"This is it," said Claude. "I came here to discover the source of my misery, and the curse imposed upon one of my children, really my entire family. I have finally come across this secret doorway that leads into a universe of secrecies cruelties beyond any man's imagination."

Claude rushed to the location where a door appeared before his eyes. Sure enough, it was a doorway covered by dead branches and leaves. He examined the mysterious door to find out that he needed a key to enter the secret domain, but where would he find it?

Standing in front of the door, Claude tried to pry open the rusty old hinges, but the door was solid and refused to give in. He walked to the wall that was now clearly visible, trying to find a week place where he could enter the mysteries hidden behind that wall.

After walking a few feet away from the entrance, Claude noticed the same trail he had followed leading him up to the targeted place had reappeared. His curiosity had reached a new level, and he decided to follow the trail; he was alert, and ready, for any sign of disturbance to happen in any minutes.

He knew that he would, at one point, must enter the combat zone that he was in the area to confront an adversary. Suddenly, just like the first time when he discovered the gate of this super hidden personal stolen garden the trail vanished.

"This must be happening for a reason," Claude reasoned. "Let's walk around here to see if there are any possible clues hidden under dead leaves, or even rocks."

Claude knelt and removed dead leaves from the ground where he was investigating; nothing had been of help so far. After a moment of reflection, He looked to his right and noticed a medium rock standing tall all by itself, like if someone, or something, had placed it there. Claude walked toward the mysterious rock with some precaution. He then decided to remove the rock out of his original location.

To Claude's surprise, the rock was easy to maneuver. He examined every inch of it with focused attention. As he was scrutinizing the rock, he stumbled upon a clue and it was letters forming, then vanishing once he had written them down. "Well," said Claude, "Let us make sense of these letters I retrieved from the rock."

He sat down not too far from the rock while he was putting the puzzle together. Here is what it said: *"You are just about to enter the kingdom of a lord but, first, you have to get the key, which is located behind the main mirror in the mansion master restroom."*

"Interesting," said Claude. "How bold this creature appears to be. If this would be a snake, I am sure he would have bitten every person who had owned this beautiful cottage."

Claude was soon out of the thick wooden area and on his way to the mansion. Rapidly approaching the family house, Claude was eager to conquer the evil that had imposed its will upon his beautiful cottage for so long. Claude inserted the key into the unlock and opened the doorknob to his mansion.

***

As soon he steeped inside, he heard the noise of shattering glass. Claude rushed to the master restroom; the main mirror was cracked from the top middle to the bottom. There was some trace of liquid spatter on the surface; it also looked like some transparent oil.

"Wow," said Claude. "What a coincidence." After he removed the broken shards of the mirror, an old key appeared. "There you are, key of miseries, and deception, of a devilish master. I am coming for you." Holding the key in his hand, Claude examined the rest of the wall; nothing appeared out of the ordinary.

After a moment, Claude had an idea. *Maybe the oil leaking from the surface of the mirror is its way of telling me to bring some oil with me. After all, every little clue like this could provide definitive details that activate positive results in a search, especially in a situation like this.*

Claude was influenced by his many years of experience dealing with supernatural events occurring here and there. He then walked over to the garage and found some light oil.

***

After that, he went back to the forest, this time with the key and oil needed for the success of his operation. Afraid, but also engulfed with positive anticipation, Claude was walking his way back to the mysterious, old, rusty door.

As he approached the trail to the targeted location, Claude's mind became overwhelmed with multiple thoughts about what could go wrong. He stayed positive throughout most of it, however, because of his taste for adventurous situations in which his odds of success are not as high as they would normally be.

***

Shortly after, he arrived back at the entry of the mysterious place after having squeezed some light oil into the lock part of the entry door. He then decided that it was time to insert the key.

Taking a deep breath, not knowing what the consequences of opening the door would be, he bravely inserted the key and try to turn open the lock. At first, it was a little difficult. Claude thought, *Well, that is totally normal. After all, how many years have passed since this lock has been turned?*

The moment of truth was about to be revealed, and it was not what Claude expected to see. Instead of witnessing a botanical paradise, all Claude could see was death, and deception, reining among the devastated garden.

Sure enough, Claude's opening the secret gate of a mysterious universe was met with a violent reaction. He heard a loud sound of thunder right after he was almost struck by lightening. The lightning had come so close to hitting him that he had seen every color design being reflected on the ground.

The sky suddenly turned gray, and the wind started to pick up so much that it looked like a tornado was forming, yet Claude's taste for adventure was not influenced. He said, "I have to confront this monster, for the sake of my younger daughter."

Carefully, and watchfully, Claude made his formal entry into the garden, and the door closed itself. He tried to reopen the door once inside the garden, but he failed in his attempt to do so. "I guess I have no choice but to confront my enemy, face-to-face. I am ready for open war with whoever, or whatever, stole this garden from the mansion."

Taking precaution, Claude ventured into the deepness of the ravaged garden. He was deeply scared of the unknown, but he knew that he had to keep going for his daughter's sake.

As Claude made his way into the forbidden garden, he was struck by a ray of light. And, in that light, Claude saw a sword and a crown. "This must be the sign that I am about to face the monster who, for so long, has terrorized this cottage."

Claude let out loud his plea, saying, "Come on, spirit, whoever you are; don't hide behind ghostly shadows. You want a confrontation, so here I am."

Seconds later, Claude saw coming toward him a dark, smoky gray centaur. After blinking his eyes, Claude was left paralyzed as the centaur approached him.

Where this will lead me? he thought. *I should have, at least, told Peter to stay far away from my excursion.* Claude now regretted his decision not to tell his friend to be at close range, just in case something would go wrong. But Claude remained strong and positive as the centaur made his way over toward him in the garden.

Now, the centaur was standing in front of him. The torso of the beast was covered up with a long, dark, gray veil. Claude noticed something very strange about the centaur's face. It was shaped more as oval as the opposite of an ordinary faces.

"What kind of monster are you?" asked Claude. "Why do you have to hide your face? You see my face, now, show me yours."

Instead of lifting his veil, he stood, immobile, while Claude was scrambling understand what he was looking at.

"That form of face is like me. I already saw you walking among us in town and eating with us at our favorite restaurant," said a nervous Claude. "What do you want from me? Are you truly PETRONAS, the magician the whole town avoided to enter into contact with?"

For the first time, the centaur spoke to Claude. "Before I remove my veil from my face, you and I will have a harsh duel." The man under the veil turned his head.

That was when Claude recognized the shape of the face, that of the librarian. "Well, what is going on here? Are you two real individuals or are you assuming personalities under the guise of a real human face?" asked Claude.

After a moment of suspense, the man under the veil turned his head toward Claude and responded, "I will tell you who *we* are. I am PETRONAS, and *she* is the town librarian. You now know more about who we are than anyone who ever searched for answers about our real identities.

"Many have come and left the haunted cottage we…" As he was about to say something more, some other figures appeared in the garden, along with other monsters. They were ugly little creatures with the face of the crazy lady, making her way toward PETRONAS.

Surprised to see the whole scenario forming, Claude now was left clueless about the next surprise that he was about to face.

As the little monsters gathered around the centaur, signaling that he was their master, PETRONAS said, "Let me finish my sentence. Yes, we own this cottage. We have been under the radar for so long that no one, except you, Claude, has come to meet any one of us face to face.

"You want to challenge me. I have heard your plea, and this is the reason why I am standing in front of you. Now that you know all our real identities, it makes no difference. Let me tell you, there will be only one who will be victorious in this battle.

"There is an all-out war situation here because you have sought to know who we are. Rest assured, I promise you, this will be a severe battle. Whoever wins this battle will be forever the master of this cottage, and the loser will be forced to surrender everything to his new master."

After a moment, Claude replied, "I am ready for an all-out war with you, PETRONAS, and your accomplices. Let me assure you, I will not sell my head that easy.

"You want to challenge me, then, let go. I will show you what my determination can perform as a father protecting his family first and then his grounds. By the way, you, crazy lady, should be ashamed for all the crimes you are the author of. Do you even have any remorse?" asked Claude.

The crazy lady replied, "Claude, it is impossible for me to have any remorse, or guilt. You hear me right because I am a double agent who used cover up to infiltrate many choices, and locations."

"Oh, I see how evil you are; you have outsmarted authorities, and other smart individuals. You have fooled an entire town, making everyone believe you are crazy. This allowed you to perpetrate orders you received from your master, PETRONAS.

"You also pretended, during multiple circumstances, that you were always at war with

PETRONAS. And I clearly remember the first day I saw you. I really did not care for your presence, especially as our closest neighbor."

The atmosphere was ripe for the eruption of the predicted battle; Claude was not willing to give in to defeat.

PETRONAS stepped in the conversation saying, "Before this goes out of hand to accelerate into a severe confrontation, I have to reveal to you other details."

Claude replied to PETRONAS, "I don't have much time to deal with you, and your army of deceivers and criminals. You know, PETRONAS, your fate is coming to an end, and I will make you pay for every dime you have caused to town to lose.

"Also, I render justice to every one of your now victims by reveling to them the truth, your lies. I will also report your multiple identities. Rest assured, once they know you, they will prosecute you, and all your accomplices."

As soon as Claude finished his last sentence, the librarian, who had so far remained quiet, jumped into the conversation saying, "Claude, there is no need to fuel the fire. It is well-lighted and could explode at any second.

"But, before you go too far and activate the scenario, I urge you to let PETRONAS finish stating his thoughts. It would only be to your advantage to sagely take my intervention into consideration.

"Just like the day you meet me at the town library, I helped you to uncover the mystery that this cottage was plagued with. I have, without the consent of PETRONAS, let you walk away with the book that guided you here today.

"So, be patient. I know PETRONAS never did forgive me for my infidelities in breaching sensitive information about all of us. That is water under the bridge but, now, it is crucial that you do not let your anger, and frustration, guiding you. That would automatically be your loss, and our gain.

"Then my question to you, dear lady," said Claude, "is why are you having a sudden change of heart? Looks to me you do not know where you are standing. Are you integral to the evil that present in such haters ready to enact any situation where devastation and sorrow become rampant?"

"Claude, I am warning you; don't be fool," replied the librarian. "I am a cruel, and very calculated, woman, a proud replica of my master, PETRONAS.

"At times, we disagree upon tactics, or means we will utilize to accomplish out our evil deeds. Nevertheless, at the end of the day, we always come out victorious."

Claude replied, "Lady, I promise to give a harsh and cruel lesson today."

After calming down, Claude addressed the monster, "Please, I am all yours, PETRONAS. Finish your thoughts before I end all this nonsense. But, let me tell you, I have never encountered such pure evil until today."

It was a very tense atmosphere. Any false movement could make the anticipated fight that PETRONAS was dragging out even longer. Everyone was in suspense, ready to execute orders from PETRONAS.

Suddenly, a bright light was observed, taking everyone by surprise.

Claude was thrown into a field of wonder, and his thoughts were going wild.

Another centaur descended from above with great majesty. A small bit of tension between Claude, PETRONAS, and the devilish army had dissipated.

Everyone was taken by surprise, especially PETRONAS, and the crazy lady, who clearly were not happy at all with the unexpected appearance.

A bright, multi-colored centaur, galloping rapidly, approached PETRONAS and his army.

As soon as PETRONAS saw this brilliant, multi-colored centaur, he let out a desperate plea,

"Go away from us! This is a personal confrontation. You do not have the right to step in uninvited!"

Claude was overjoyed at the sight of PETRONAS appearing vulnerable, stepping down from his arrogance, and superiority.

The crazy lady removed herself from the path of the centaur who was now approaching amazingly fast, ready to trample any object, or obstacle, standing in his way.

"Oh, no!" screamed the librarian. "We are all bound to be defeated with the arrival of our number one enemy."

With that said, Claude knew that the multi-colored centaur was, most likely, his ally. Claude finally felt that he had something going in his favor among these monsters.

Sure enough, the bright creature galloped toward Claude then knelt down as if he is telling Claude to not be afraid.

At that moment, Claude was projected onto the bust of the centaur, and he automatically became a centaur, himself.

The centaur majestically stood back up again. Then, the conversation continued with Claude, who was now as a centaur.

A proud Claude, empowered by the latest event, addressed PETRONAS. "Now that I am a centaur, myself. I see you are more cautious, and less prompt to dare me into entering your safety zone before you had this advantage over me."

A more reserved PETRONAS responded, "Yes, dear friend, I did not expect this unpredicted event to come and shield you from my evil."

Having said that, the librarian replied, "PETRONAS, don't give Claude the pleasure of seeing our vulnerability. Instead, let us confront him with all of our might."

During the conversation, Claude had a vision instructing him what to do, and what to look for.

Claude seemed distant for a while, which made PETRONAS presumptuous. PETRONAS tried to approach the multicolored centaur to benefit from the perfect moment to attack Claude but, before he could come close to doing so, he was rebuked fiercely by the multicolored centaur.

Claude was collecting, in order, the information that the multi-colored centaur gave him. First, he had to remove the gray veil from PETRONAS. Then, the real reason why the veil was covering PETRONAS' face would come to light.

What would follow was an attack from the little monsters and the crazy lady, coming forward to defend their master, whom Claude would have to kill for him to dissolve into thin air.

PETRONAS, and the librarian, would follow with a massive attack. And, at that precise moment, Claude would have to pull PETRONAS's veil and remove the crown which the beast was furiously fighting to keep hidden.

After that, Claude's victory would follow, and PETRONAS, along with the librarian, would vanish into thin air. Claude was instructed to be very gentle with the crown. That would be a hard task for him while fighting against PETRONAS and his army of monsters, but he knew that failure was not an option.

Chapter 11
The Curse is Broken

Claude was ready for the ultimate battle against his adversary, who possessed the answer for the deliverance of his daughter. He could not wait for one more second to engage in the duel. Claude was now in position to accelerate the process.

It took just a little bit of time for Claude to manoeuvre himself as a centaur. That was an experience he never had dreamed of having before, facing his advisory vested with the agility of a centaur. Armed with the sword which appeared with the crown in the ray of light, Claude was now ready for action.

PETRONAS, on the other hand, appeared not so willing to engage with Claude as he pulled out his sword from under the veil covering his face.

The moment of truth was about to become reality. As soon PETRONAS put his hand on his sword, the crazy lady made of the little monsters approached Claude. She gave a signal to her partner in crime, indicating that it was their time to attack Claude.

A violent response followed the signal given. It was an all-out war situation. Claude was surrounded with bunch of hideous creatures who were going after his centaur leg. His defence was to kick sideways, front ways, and back ways and step on those beasts until they died. It was not an easy task for the newly unexperienced centaur.

Claude appeared to be winning the battle. One after another, he succeeded to crush the little monsters coming at him with all their rage.

The last part of the fight would directly involve the crazy lady. Claude could wait to crush her down. He could not wait to put her in her place, especially because he believed that she had something to do with the curse cast upon his younger daughter.

Now he was given the opportunity not only to confront the ugly creature but also eradicate her from the face of the Earth. But before doing so, he would ask her a couple questions about what she knew and her part in his daughter's misfortune.

Claude saw the crazy lady approaching him, and he screamed at her, "Before you come any closer, I want you to tell me your part in the curse cast unto my daughter, Myriam."

The crazy lady replied, "Your daughter is the one who cast upon herself her own curse. Everyone was warned to not remove the blindfold from the doll, but her curiosity pushed her to do so."

That was not the answer Claude was waiting for from the miserable creature. How could she place the blame on his daughter for her taste for adventure? "Tell me why you allowed a doll to be cursed," said a furious Claude.

PETRONAS was supervising the confrontation, but he stayed neutral. He wanted to know everything that Claude had come to discover, or knew, about the whole scenario.

Now, Claude was galloping, a centaur charging at the little ugly creature.

Shortly after, Claude had all the little monsters surrender, trying to get to bite the leg of his centaur. With energy, Claude defended himself from the bites from the small teeth of those cruel and vicious creatures.

He was at war with an army of evil spirits under the guidance of their master, the crazy lady, and she was under scrutiny of her master PETRONAS.

One after the another, they all succumbed to Claude's determination. He knew who his real target was; the little servants had to give their lives before he got to their master.

Finally, after great effort, Claude gained control over the situation, and the crazy lady was left by herself to confront a determined Claude.

"Now, it is your turn, my dear, little, ugly, good-for-nothing creature," said Claude. "Let's see how brave you now that all your supporters are dead and lying under my centaur feet."

The crazy lady gave PETRONAS a look and said, "PETRONAS, remember what I told you earlier. Now, it is my turn to get crushed by the determination of Claude, but do not you worry. You will be the next one to endure a big defeat."

Claude already savored the death of the monster. He was already making plans to overthrow PETRONAS and remove the veil from his torso to see what he was hiding, and protecting, with his own life.

Claude knew that it was something directly involving in the healing of his daughter, as he recalled seeing the short vision which warned him that confrontation was well on its way.

Claude said, "I just can't wait to defeat you, crazy lady, and charge you, PETRONAS. Your little peons have to be brought to death before the real monster finally must face justice."

With that said, Claude launched himself, in a furious rage, upon the ugly creature whom the crazy lady used to confront him.

She responded, with vigor, at every attempt that Claude was imposing on her until she was cornered with no place to go but to surrender. Claude took the sword he had received at the very beginning of the confrontation and finally executed the monster creature.

The crazy lady let out a sound of despair and rage as she dissolved in thin air, leaving behind no remains.

At that precise moment, PETRONAS entered the battlefield. This time, it was two centaurs against each other, one evil and the other good.

Claude remained focused; he had to succeed in tearing off PETRONAS's veil and retrieving what was hidden under it. It was not an easy task, but it was not an impossible one, either.

The beginning of the fight with PETRONAS was a warm-up between the two centaurs. For Claude, it gave him the confidence to confront someone who had advantages over him.

Then, PETRONAS gave the signal for the cruel confrontation. He exclaimed, "Well, Claude, let's see who will be triumphant. You will repay me, and all my beloved army, if I overthrow you. Also, I will surrender you as one of the ugly evil creatures."

Claude was not about to take that nonsense challenge. He proclaimed, "And I will make you pay for all the evil that you are responsible for in this town, including the condition that you put upon my daughter. I shall put you on trial. I will enjoy seeing you dying a long and cruel death. I will torture you mentally. Don't underestimate me because, when you pushed me at the end of my rope, I also became cruel and vindictive."

Claude's response made the atmosphere even tenser and was now at a boiling point.

PETRONAS accelerated toward Claude.

Claude's sword was in his hand as he wisely studied the easiest way to retrieve the veil covering PETRONAS and the librarian. Another threat for Claude was the fact that the PETRONAS centaur had the ability to change personality at the speed of light.

The librarian replied, "And I will make you my personal slave, and I shall be to you, as you have killed my best friend, the crazy lady."

To that, Claude replied, "Thank you for the heads up, dear librarian, and I will make sure that the whole town knows the monster you always were behind the front desk of the town library.

"You thought that you would get away for your part in covering up crime that was inflicted on this peaceful town. Let me tell you, it will be exactly the opposite. I will render your life so miserable that you will wish that you never came to know me."

The war of the words was coming to an end as the fire between good and evil could be felt all along the atmosphere. The timing was never so ripe for a confrontation. The PETRONAS centaur stomped furiously on the ground.

Claude, on the other hand, was utilizing common sense, every second developing a wise strategy to overthrow PETRONAS. He had only one motive to take on the challenge.

After a couple more rounds, PETRONAS finally decided to initiate the attack. He suddenly rushed toward the Claude centaur, and the war was declared.

Claude, armed with the sword that appeared with the crown in the ray of light, was responding, with precision, to every sharp attack made by PETRONAS.

Claude had the advantage because of his reputation of being a good shot once he had a target in mind; he never missed, as he was known as a professional rifle handler. Working with a sword was a little different for Claude. Nevertheless, he was good at projecting every shot that he flung toward PETRONAS.

No one spoke a word while the two centaurs were battling; there was so much action coming from all directions. It was tense, and cruel, moment.

With all his heart, Claude yearned for Myriam's deliverance from the curse; the entire family was suffering. Claude keep his daughter in mind with every blow that PETRONAS had struck. Myriam's visage reminded him to stay strong, and vigilant.

While going hard at it, Claude noticed that the wind had lifted the veil covering the torso of the PETRONAS centaur. He was studying, while fighting against PETRONAS's attacks, how to remove the veil without breaking whatever PETRONAS had hidden underneath.

Since Claude has no idea what the veil was underneath, he could only imagine that it was a crown. He knew that he had to succeed to retrieve what PETRONAS kept under his veil without breaking it. Claude was aware that, whatever it was, could be easily broken.

From time to time, the metal of two swords contacted each other while the two opponents were already calculating their next move.

At the beginning of the fight, PETRONAS was full of himself. Never did he even consider that

Claude was a champion of manoeuvres that involved such rapidity, and precision. Claude never missed his chance when PETRONAS showed signs of weakness.

The librarian was to coach her partner in crime; she was the one who secretly told PETRONAS Claude's intentions. At one point, she let out the secret which motivated Claude to execute a strong and professional move with the precision of an athlete.

She reminded PETRONAS just how important it was to keep the veil covering the torso of their centaur. "If Claude were to see underneath the veil, it would be the end of both of us, as we would have to surrender to him the art of knowledge."

To that, PETRONAS exclaimed, "Now I see what you are up to, my dear adversary! Let me tell you, I knew, all along, what your plans were. And, so far, I have succeeded to defeat every one of you moves."

Just as PETRONAS was bragging about his success, the perfect storm was forming against him. Nature was rebelling against evil, and it aligned with the courage and perseverance of a father who was giving everything he had to rescue one of his daughters.

"Oh, no," said the librarian. "PETRONAS let's hurry and get this battle over with. It looks like nature is siding with Claude. Look how much the wind has pick up just in a few seconds; it is already unbearable. We have to win this; otherwise, we will be reduced to giving up and returning to where we came from."

PETRONAS responded by putting more pressure onto Claude in order to force him to fall victim, or simply give up the fight.

Claude was struggling so much that he was just about to lose the battle. PETRONAS had changed his tactics aggressively, but Claude did not give up because his goal was still clear in his mind. If he gave up, he would have to surrender everything to PETRONAS last effort to overthrow him.

At the most crucial moment of his mortal engagement, Claude noticed a rainbow in the sky; it seemed to give him supernatural strength. He vowed that he would win because of his newfound strength.

The wind became so strong that even the dead trees of the garden were strongly shaken to the point that Claude thought, for a moment, that a tornado was approaching.

PETRONAS had a hard time maneuvering his centaur; he was exhausted from fighting Claude. And the latter of the two knew that he would succeed in his delicate mission to retrieve the mysterious object that PETRONAS kept hidden under his dark green veil.

PETRONAS was all too aware of his vulnerabilities. As for the librarian, she already knew that it was a lost situation for both if the wind did not calm down.

Nevertheless, PETRONAS decided not to surrender so easily, although nature was working against him. He gave everything he had to curb, and steal, the victory from Claude. However, nothing was working; PETRONAS was becoming increasingly vulnerable.

Claude noticed that PETRONAS was struggling with the amount of wind that nature was providing to help Claude defeat his evil foe. Claude was not about to let PETRONAS, or any of his accomplices', crimes go unaccounted for.

The moment for justice had sounded, and the clock was ticking forward judgment; no one could stop it. Claude was the chosen one to rectify the situation and bring peace back to the lovely cottage for many years to come.

But, for now, the reality was that Claude was not out of the woods yet. PETRONAS and the librarian dished out everything that they had.

"I believe this is our last chance," said the librarian. "We are in this fight to win, and shall we succeed; we will be forever the king among future owner of this cottage."

Upon hearing the last sentence, Claude replied, "And I'm in for the win also to crush your evil, reduce your clairvoyance, and remove the curse from my younger daughter."

As PETRONAS was approaching Claude for what appeared to be his last daring shot, the wind became suddenly unbearable.

Claude's centaur had a hard time just staying focused while walking toward his adversary.

It took everything in PETRONAS's might to keep his balance while daring Claude's centaur to come closer.

At that precise moment, Claude had the perfect opportunity. The wind had lifted the dark gray veil covering PETRONAS's torso just enough for Claude to witness that it was, in fact, a wonderful crown that PETRONAS was furiously protecting.

Claude knew that it was his moment to overthrow PETRONAS and make him surrender to his authority.

For a while, the situation was looking chaotic for PETRONAS, as the forces of nature sowed her disapproval, and disgust, toward such evil. Then Claude, with the tip of his sword, attempted to go under the long gray veil covering the torso of the PETRONAS centaur.

The wind lifted the corner of the veil, which allowed Claude to make an attempt at great success. He succeeded in going under PETRONAS's without tearing it; he held the veil at the center.

The PETRONAS centaur continued to move forward and, soon, Claude had removed the veil covering the torso of the PETRONAS centaur.

Now with the veil removed from the PETRONAS's centaur's torso, PETRONAS could not stand the bright the light of day. His focus had failed to give Claude just enough time to finally have PETRONAS under his sword.

Before piercing the heart of the centaur of PETRONAS, Claude cornered the beast so well that PETRONAS was not able to respond to Claude preciseness.

With precaution, Claude lifted the beautiful crown out from under PETRONAS's veil.

The beast let out a loud cry of distress.

The librarian was also in agony. "This is it, PETRONAS! We have lost our battle and, now, we will lose everything that we have had for so long. I thought you were invincible. I joined you on your promise you will never be defeated and, now, look at you. Better yet, look at us."

PETRONAS furiously replied to his partner in crime, "You know, my dear, we have fought hard all along and, today, we are cast out of our domain. This is the unthinkable scenario that I never saw coming.

"I must admit, I wasn't prepared to face Claude's determination. As for the promise I made to you, no one will get close to me. It does matter anymore; we lost our power the second that Claude removed the crown from me."

PETRONAS yelled at Claude with rage, "And you are the first one that challenged me directly. You are the victor, and your daughter shall be rendered to you whole again.

"Now, go ahead initiate my end, cease my misery so I can depart this world." PETRONAS spat at Claude while waiting for the final blow that would cost him his life, and the life of the librarian, his partner in crime.

With a smile on his face, Claude replied, "PETRONAS, your evil will be put to an end, once and for all. You shall never be allowed to come back to this beautiful community. I shall render your name public, and your life of deception will be published so that everyone who comes to live in this town knows that, once upon a time, you were causing death and despair."

PETRONAS could say nothing, and the librarian saw Claude gluing her picture right above the front desk where she uses to sat quietly while protecting PETRONAS's, and the crazy lady's, real identities. She was furious as well, anticipating the moment Claude when would release their fictional lives out into the public.

After taking one last look PETRONAS, and his accomplice, Claude finally pierced the PETRONAS centaur right in his heart.

At that moment, the beast made his dying scream, which was so loud that it could heard all the throughout the town. Then, suddenly, he vanished into thin air.

Claude knew that PETRONAS, along with his accomplice in crime, was forever dead. He felt PETRONAS's spirit swivel in the air, like a furious lion reduced to silence.

Claude took the crown, examined the precious ornament to ensure that there was no curse left on it, and put it onto his head.

At that moment. the multi-colored centaur was kneeling back down, letting Claude know that it was time for him to say goodbye.

After having given a huge hug to the multi-colored centaur, his saviour, with tears running down his face, Claude witnessed the creature disappear the same way he made his appearance.

"This is one experience I will never forget," said Claude.

After many hours in direct combat with PETRONAS, and his partners in crime, Claude had finally gained the upper hand. The curse imposed upon the cottage all those years ago was lifted at last.

Now, with the crown at his disposal, he was proud to bring his trophy home to share the good new with his family, and the rest of the town.

After the challenge was over, Claude witnessed the garden regaining life. What once appeared dead was rejuvenated just as enhancement filled all the flowers as they bloomed and gave off their natural perfume.

"Wow!" exclaimed Claude. "I couldn't have wished a better welcome from nature after having cleared the Earth of those monsters." A beautiful lake was appearing where was once there was an uninhabitable desert.

Chapter 12
The Reward

During that time, Sophia, along with the rest of the children, were wondering where Claude had been all day. The day was almost over, and it was not typical of him to leave without telling them what he was doing, or where he was going to be.

The doctor was performing his daily health checkup on Myriam, and there were some new developments. He called Sophia to tell her that Myriam's vital signs were stronger they were some progress made by stating, "Myriam is not out of the woods yet. However, it looks like she is healing."

Sophia was pleased to hear the doctor's diagnosis of her younger daughter. "So, are you telling me that, soon, we will be able to transfer Myriam from this miserable place to her bed at the mansion?" asked Sophia.

"Yes, I am positive about this," replied the doctor. "If things continue to get better, I am almost certain that she will come out of her coma."

Upon hearing that good news, Sophia put aside her concerns about her husband. She was happy to hear something so positive. "Whatever it will take to get my daughter back to her family, I am ready to do," said Sophia.

***

During that time, Claude was walking home with the crown on his head. "This crown was the missing piece to the puzzle," said Claude. "I am sure there will be some more instructions given to me about what to do with it. Maybe there is a part in the book that will talk about a crown."

After having carefully inspected the ornament, Claude was pleased about the latest developments that provided him the opportunity to confront, and destroy, his adversaries.

The whole town was on alert because, while Claude administrated the last blow to PETRONAS, the beast had let out a sinisterly loud noise that was heard all the way across the island, where Sophia and the children stayed by the side of their sibling.

When the children heard that noise, they all ran for cover, Sophia was on the lookout, especially for Myriam, who was still under the strange spell.

The police were dispatched throughout the entire village, and the nearby buildings where they thought the criminals were hiding. Some of the police were sent to the mansion to ensure that no other problems were observed and/or recorded.

The train was on its way back to town after having vanished for a good couple of days, and Claude was able to witness the slow moving of the famed locomotive.

"There is our train," said Claude. "Now I know that I succeeded to break the curse cast upon this beautiful place." Claude was not aware that the whole town was on high alert and, when he reached his mansion, he was taken by surprise to see so many officers around.

As he approached his family home, many of the officers were surprised to see Claude, not aware of the reason for their presence.

Some officers noticed that Claude was wearing a crown on his head, but no one felt comfortable enough to ask him why.

Claude carefully placed the crown onto high shelves and told the officer that he needed to talk to the family doctor. He was wondering if he already had come to render his daily visit to Myriam.

"Yes," replied one officer. "As a matter of fact, he just left a couple minutes ago and told me that he was driving to his office."

"Thank you so much," replied Claude. "It is important that I speak to him before he goes home."

The officer replied, "Go on, then. We will ensure that no one messes with your home. We've been here for a couple of hours already, since the scary noise was heard all over the town."

"What noise are you talking about?" asked Claude.

The officer responded, "It sounded like someone was murdered not too terribly far from your domain."

"Okay, I have to go. I will tell you everything you need to know on my way back." Then, Claude entered his car and drove to the family doctor's office.

***

Just as he pulled into the driveway of the clinic, the doctor was on his way out. Claude called him from his vehicle window and asked him if he could have a few moments to talk with him.

"Yes, Claude, I will always find some time for you, and your family; how I may help you?"

After warm handshake, Claude told the doctor about the experience he just had during the past couple of hours as he came face-to-face with the author of the curse imposed on Myriam.

"That's good to know," replied the doctor. "For some unknown reason, your daughter has made some progress during the time of your absence. It lasted until I left the island just over one hour ago, and I am sure that she will continue to feel the same way after my departure. Her vital signs were stronger, and some of her reflexes are coming back. It is encouraging to see the sudden progress, and I am so pleased to announce this to you."

"Thank you so much for the good news, doctor. I believe that I possess the piece of the puzzle we are missing for the deliverance of my younger daughter. We will talk about this tomorrow. I just wanted to tell you these details; I believe they are extremely important."

"Have a great night," replied the doctor. "First thing in the morning I will be at your door."

"That sounds like a plan to me. I, myself, must go before my wife, and children, start to panic. I was gone since this morning and, now, it almost supper time," replied Claude.

Claude drove straight back to the family mansion.

***

Sure enough, Sophia and the children were already back home, relieved that they already had someone to take over guarding Myriam for the night.

Sophia was happy to see her husband for the very first time that day. She knew where he was because Peter came to let her know a little bit about the ordeal Claude involved himself with. She told Claude that Peter let her know that everything would be all right.

"This is true, and I told Peter to tell you these things so you did not panic," replied Claude. "What a frightening, exciting day. What I had to deal with today was like nothing that I never before dreamt would become a reality for me."

Sophia listened intently to every word that her husband was telling her. "Tell me more about this experience you had; I am dying to hear about it."

Julian walked into his parents' room to let them know that he was about to take a shower then head off to bed. The rest of Julian's siblings would go to sleep soon as well.

"Sounds good, Son," replied Claude. "In the meantime, your mother and I will have to have a little conversation."

"Not a problem, Dad. I know my siblings are tired from their stressful day," said Julian. "They will be quiet, and in bed, shortly after they take their showers."

Julian walked to his room, gathered what he needed for his shower time than walked toward the bathroom. To his surprise, he noticed that the main mirror was removed and, for some reason, set aside along the toilet wall. He also noticed that the mirror was cracked from top to bottom, like someone had hit it with a baseball bat.

Taken off guard, Julian screamed in horror, "Dad, Mom, please, hurry! I believe we are all in deep trouble."

Hearing her elder son's plea, Sophia was the first one who arrived to see what the matter was.

After witnessing the horror, Sophia said, "Oh, my dear, let us all go to a motel for the night. I believe that they are coming for all of us. Who in their right mind would mess with the main mirror in the bathroom?"

Claude did not expect this to occur. He knew who did it, and why, but he simply forgot about it.

Then, there was a general panic in the mansion; everyone, except Claude, was traumatized by Julian's discovery.

"Please, calm down. Let me explain to you what happened earlier this morning," said Claude. It took him a great amount of energy, and persuasion, to finally succeed in calming down every one of his dear family.

Claude then remembered that, for a good couple of months, the mansion was nothing, but a burden filled with misery: Myriam was paralyzed because of a haunted doll which belonged to the crazy lady.

Also, PETRONAS dispensed terror, day in and day out. It was enough to wear them all down. For the children, it was a constant dilemma to see their younger sister turned into wax, unable to walk, run, and play with them.

Claude finally succeeded in convincing everyone to stay at the family mansion for the night. After all, he was the one who removed the mirror earlier.

Before going to bed, Sophia made a round to each door to ensure that their safety locks were in their position. She simply could not deal with another family tragedy.

The atmosphere of peace and tranquility returned to normal, and the children took their showers before settling into their beds for the night. The beauty of the silence made Claude feel joyful, and at peace. He finally had succeeded in overthrowing PETRONAS and his army of evil little monster creatures.

Sophia was unaware of the crown which Claude had retrieved from PETRONAS. As she climbed into bed, she suddenly spotted the object. It was stored up so high that she had a hard time making out what it was. All she knew was that it was something that had not there before. Out of curiosity, Sophia asked her husband if he knew anything about the crown.

After a moment Claude replied, "Yes, I actually do. The crown came to me with a price, and I have received specific orders to follow. If one of them is breached, then we could land ourselves in a different situation."

When Sophia formed a confused look, Claude continued. "The good luck of our family will come when Myriam heals from the curse imposed on her. I promise you, Sophia, I will always put the safety of our children first and, as for Myriam, I sometimes beat myself against the wall because she got her taste for adventure, and challenging situations, from me."

After a brief exchange, Claude and Sophia fell asleep. Nothing out of the ordinary happened, except that Claude and Sophia had the same exact dream at the exact same time.

***

The morning arrived, and the children were already up and running. Claude and Sophia were still in bed, relaying the dream that they both had. They could not believe that they both had the dream the same time.

"Claude, we both dreamed, at the same time, that the crown you retrieved from PETRONAS's head was actually the precious metal that will render our daughter safe and sound."

"Yes," replied Claude. "But there is just a little detail that you missed. We have to put the crown onto Myriam's head as she wakes up from the curse. The famous doll will appear next to her."

The couple did not know what to think about that part of the dream. However, they were at peace with the idea of seeing this doll enter their home.

"Maybe this doll will become Myriam and Jessica's best friend. I am sure that, if this doll comes back, the curse imposed on her would dissolve," said Sophia.

"That makes perfect sense, Sophia," said Claude.

The children ran into their parents' room. They wanted to let them know that they were all right and they had sweet dreams, the likes of which they never had before.

Jessica even talked about a similar dream Claude and Sophia have had exited to tell the dream she had about her younger daughter. "That's a good sign Sophia," said Claude. "Now, let's get breakfast ready and tackle this new day," said the enthusiastic father.

After they had finished breakfast, the joyous family prepared what personal belongings they would need during their day at the island.

Sophia prepared a lunch for the mid-day snack.

Claude told Sophia that he wanted the doctor present while they executed the dream which both they and Jessica had.

"That sounds like a great idea," replied Sophia. "In the meantime, I will walk down to the island, hopefully for the last time."

***

Sophia, once more, found herself in the shack on the middle of the island as Claude loaded up the crown and drove off to the doctor's office.

***

He arrived on time, as the doctor was just about to drive off to render a visit to Myriam.

The doctor saw Claude pull in and waited for him to walk toward his car. After a brief exchange, they agreed to meet on the island.

Claude drove slowly so that the doctor could follow. Something was telling Claude that his family nightmare was about to be resolved.

Both men arrived at the island at the same time, and they walked to the shack together.

Once the two men arrived, they noticed, right away, that Myriam was looking a lot better, as if she were almost out of her coma. Claude ran to his car, retrieved the famous crown, and came right back into the shack. It was the first time ever the children had seen it; they were mystified.

Before anyone could touch the crown, Claude gently lifted up Myriam's head as the doctor lowered the crown onto it.

Sophia was anticipating the end of her nightmare because of the dream she had about the crown.

As soon the crown was perfectly situated onto Myriam's head, she miraculously recovered from her curse.

The child smiled as she called out to her parents. Tears streamed down all their faces as Myriam's siblings rushed to give her a huge hug. It was a touching moment.

Just as Claude thought, the doll appeared almost immediately in her original form and, yes, she was extremely beautiful.

Myriam exclaimed, "Here you are, my dear friend! I was trying to rescue you from danger and, now, you appear in front of us as, just as saw you the first time."

Myriam hugged her newfound friend as she climbed out of the bed for the first time since the beginning of her whole ordeal.

The doctor conducted a few tests to see if everything was normal, and Myriam looked like nothing bad had happened to her.

At that precise moment when Myriam stood up from her rustic bed, a gentle, bright light emanated from the secret garden.

The whole town witnessed the peaceful, bright light coming out of nowhere, shining upon an area that, for so long, was under a spell of devastation.

Everything in the cottage was renewed. The train was where it always was stationed, shining beautifully, just like before the curse has been cast onto the cottage.

The sawmill area, and the powerhouse, became clean of the dead branches and mold that accumulated near the building over a long period of time. Everything was rejuvenated, and the whole town felt like a great weight had just been lifted. There were no more crazy ladies, and everyone just now had put the pieces of puzzle together.

A couple of officers made a brief visit to the cottage to ensure that no intruders had made their way onto the property.

The joyous family entered their home sweet home, this time accompanied by Myriam, who miraculously, did not recall any of her time while she was under PETRONAS and the crazy lady's spell.

The secret garden became famous after Claude revealed to the whole town about both its dark side, and its bright side. The train was, once again, at the disposition of the whole town, providing the transportation which they missed dearly.

At night, Claude and his family, with some of their friends and neighbors, set out on their way to the wonder of nature to witness the sun going down for the night and the moon taking over, along with the company of millions of stars shining under a calm, and celestial, blue sky.

Claude's family spent numerous quality years together, enjoying the curse-free mansion. Everyone now wanted to acquire this masterpiece of nature, and the price of the property was as sky high from the very first day that it became inhabitable.

Claude and Sophia were proud parents whose career was growing, every day, since Claude had finally succeeded in putting to rest the curse the cottage was plagued with.

Claude never ran out of jobs; everyone was asking for his feedback, and the knowledge that he had acquired over years of working in the field of paranormal situations.

 **Author Joseph Daeges** has lived in Omaha, Nebraska since 1997. Before moving to Omaha, he lived in Canada, where he spent his entire childhood. Some of his interests include taking walks in the woods, fishing, and hanging out with his friends and family. Joseph also enjoys quiet time spent at home, letting his imagination be free to navigate. This allows him to write down thoughts and memories about all the good times he's had. Joseph's favorite books include adventure, history, and paranormal documentations. He very much enjoys visiting the zoo in Omaha, Nebraska, which is a perfect architecture of knowledge, and care, for animals. It is a must see for anyone who visits the beautiful city of Omaha.

Milton Keynes UK
Ingram Content Group UK Ltd.
UKHW022158030324
438776UK00012B/1807